DISARMING THE RANCHER

BARB HAN

TORJAKE PUBLISHING

Editing: Ali Williams

Cover Design: Jacob's Cover Designs

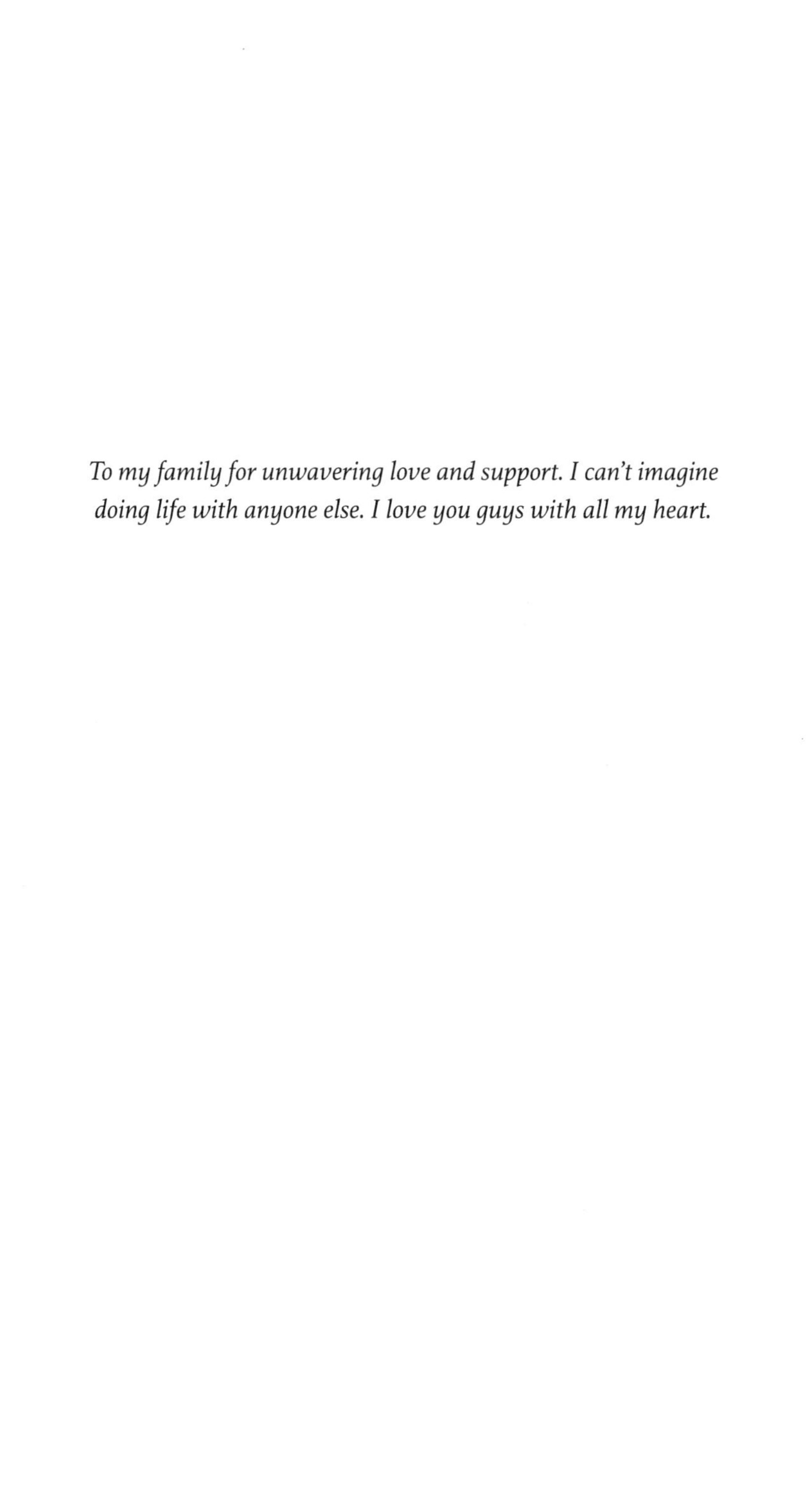

To my family for unwavering love and support. I can't imagine doing life with anyone else. I love you guys with all my heart.

1

Raleigh Perry couldn't wait for a shower larger than thirty-four inches. The one in the tour bus was like showering in a casket. Sharing said shower with eight others was next to impossible, but the band decided it would be safer to stick together during the crisis. She sat staring out the window in anticipation. Seeing her nana's house—*her* house since Nana's passing two years ago—again brought a flood of good memories from a happy childhood. But even those couldn't help her shake the dark cloud hanging over her head after the bomb threat that was sending her home in the first place. The threat had turned out to be real when an explosive was found taped underneath the stage. If it had been allowed to go off, the band, the road crew, and many of the band's most loyal fans would have been killed. Raleigh shuddered thinking about what might have happened, grateful no one got hurt.

She forced those memories aside, needing a break from the stress of what might have been along with the guilt of letting her fans down for dropping out of the tour. Not one time in almost fourteen years of touring had she canceled a show, let alone for the foreseeable future.

On a sharp sigh, Raleigh gave herself a mental head-shake. The anticipation of seeing those serene five acres with bluebonnet-dotted fields was building, tickling her stomach and she desperately needed to clear her head to stop churning over all the *what ifs*.

The all-white siding, wooden shudders, and grass-green tin roof on the two-story farmhouse was the only home Raleigh had ever known. She'd spent countless hours in a rocker on the wrap-around porch with nothing more than a pick and a guitar to entertain herself. Nana had kept the place in pristine condition. Fresh linens on the bed, fresh flowers in the kitchen. And she had those massive ferns hanging on the porch that was on every picture of a porch in the southwest. She'd been a stickler for cleanliness and order and had provided the structure Raleigh needed after coming to live there at six-years-old.

Looking back, Nana had never discussed the circumstances in which she'd come to raise her only granddaughter. Raleigh had been too young to remember, but she didn't have any bad will toward her absentee parents. Her mother had died when Raleigh was a baby and her father tried for six years to work and keep her before dropping her off at Nana's. That was as much as Raleigh knew. She'd never felt the need to find her father and he must have felt the same. She had no idea the conditions in which she lived her first six years of life and no one to tell her about them. It was strange when she thought about it in those terms. Her first six years were a blank canvas.

Having a person like Nana had more than made up for her father's absence.

"We must be getting close," she said under her breath.

Granted, she hadn't been back in two years, but she should recognize something at this point. There was more to Nana's place than the overgrown weeds that stretched out as far as the eye could see.

"How much longer does GPS think until we get there, Buck?" she asked her tour bus driver. Henry Buckner had been her road manager since day one. He was the closest thing to a father she'd ever known.

"Says we're basically here," he said.

"How?" She blinked as Nana's home came into view, or at least part of it. She could barely see past the tall grass that was supposed to be cut on a regular basis. Paint on the white fence was chipped. The shudders on the home were closed, just as she'd last left them. "What the heck?"

Raleigh palmed her cell and hit Wade's name on her recent calls list as her blood pressure kicked up a few notches.

"Everything okay?" The fear in his voice was a stark reminder of what they'd just been through at the last venue.

"Yes. We're fine. I'm fine. Everything is fine. Physically. But what happened to the house and property I inherited?" She got straight to the point since he was supposed to be keeping the place up for her while she was on the road.

"The what?" he hedged, and she could hear something that sounded a lot like guilt in his voice.

"Don't play games with me." Her voice came out a little more curt than she'd intended but this was Nana's place and she would have had a heart attack if she'd still been alive. "You're my business manager, Wade. You came to the funeral with me and then told me to get back on the road and sing, which I did. Because you assured me that everything would be taken care. As far as I can recall, the last time I brought this place up, you assured me again that it was being cared for. And then you told me it was in great shape. This subject has come up at every monthly financial meeting, so don't pretend like you suddenly don't know what I'm talking about."

"You're right." He immediately changed his tune. "All I can do is apologize at this point. I should have been taking better care of your property."

She didn't correct him to say her nana's property. She would always think of it in those terms though.

"However," he quickly added, "right now I'm in the middle of rescheduling your tour and working with the FBI to figure out what's going on and stop this sonofabitch from pulling anything like this again. So, forgive me if I'm caught off guard when because someone isn't mowing when they're supposed to."

A cell phone's ringtone sounded in the background.

"I need to take this," he said on a sharp sigh and she could hear the stress in his voice. "Sorry for letting you down, Raleigh. I truly am."

There was so much heaviness in those words, she decided to ease up on her business manager.

"All right. I'll figure something out here," she said before exchanging goodbyes and ending the call. Considering Wade handled all her finances, business and personal, she was left wondering what other balls he might be dropping. His cousin Sharon had started out on this journey with Raleigh and stayed up until four years ago when she met the man of her dreams and they decided to start a family. Sharon was gold and had been a dear friend. She'd trained Wade on handling the business so as not to leave Raleigh high and dry, which had been much appreciated. Wade wasn't Sharon though. Cracks were beginning to show in his management skills. There were times when he was late paying the road crew, which was unacceptable. And now this? She had the feeling she was going to have to be a lot more hands-on when it came to managing her band's career and financing.

When was there time? A little voice in the back of her mind picked that moment to speak up. It was true. She'd been touring or in the studio nonstop since she started.

Buck pulled up alongside the house. The rocking chairs had been tipped over on their sides. There were no ferns hanging. Although, that wasn't as unexpected. Generally speaking, the whole place looked neglected and it broke her heart.

"This the right place?" Buck asked. He was as loyal as they came. He was incredible at his job. The man could set up and break down a stage in record time and required very little in the way of help. Too bad he didn't know anything about business or she'd hire him to replace Wade. Buck had the kind of loyalty that didn't come around often.

She stood up and walked behind the driver's seat of the bus.

"I'm afraid so. We'll get a spit-shine on the place in no time." She squeezed Buck's shoulder as he put the gearshift in park.

Buck turned his chair around to face inside the bus as Raleigh stepped in front of the exit door. "Okay, we all know we're going to be living here for the next two weeks. Less if they can find the guy..." She paused as she searched all seven faces starting at her, stopping on Hardy Blake's, her full-time security guard. The reality they could be sticking around a lot longer was evident on his stone face. "We need to make the best of the hand we've been dealt."

Heads nodded, except Kenny. He stood in the back of

the bus, leaning his hip against the counter, staring at the tile.

"It's nothing a lawn mower won't fix," Jake said with his usual optimism. He was the youngest on the tour and worked directly for Buck.

"Leave it to Johnny on the Spot," Kenny whispered and Tim rolled his eyes. Her drummer and fiddle player could be hard on the greenhorn.

"Sorry, I didn't hear that, Kenny. Do you want to speak a little louder so everyone can be in on the joke?" She and Kenny spent the first two years on the road as an on-again, off-again couple until she'd put her foot down. They were either together, or they weren't. His choice. But if he picked her, the other women had to go. He'd pledged his love and that had worked for about a month, until she popped into his dressing room unexpectedly before a show and caught him red-handed. Or, should she say pants down?

That was all water under the bridge now, but had ripped her heart out of her chest at the time. Then, like now, she had to put her personal feelings aside and kept trucking.

Recently, she'd overheard him tell Tim that she was the one who got away and now that his divorce was final, he had plans to win her back. She might be in a dating drought, but she had no desire to walk down that worn path again.

"I think Jake was trying to say that with a little elbow grease, this place will be in shape in no time," Buck said. Everyone respected the oldest guy on the tour.

"Follow me." Raleigh forced a smile, stuffing down how much her heart hurt at seeing the condition of the place she loved. She grabbed her cell and her handbag, fumbling around for the key. It was broad daylight in the middle of June, so there'd be plenty of sunshine to work with while they spruced the place up. Besides, they'd been antsy on the bus during the drive over. Everyone needed a way to work off some of the frustration and fear of being someone's target.

They'd been through a traumatic experience and they were tired. Heck, she was tired. She'd been daydreaming about going for a walk on pristine grounds half the drive over. Maybe sitting outside and finding the reset button after the night before last's unsettling events.

However, work kept the mind busy. It might not be what anyone wanted, least of all her, but it would probably be good for every last one of them.

She led the group inside the house. After the two-cent tour, she walked into the kitchen and grabbed a broom.

Willie opened the fridge. Her back-up guitar player was always hungry. The stench elicited a chorus of groans.

"No power," he said.

More groans filled the room as Raleigh opened a window.

"Relax. Nana has a generator. That'll get us through the night until I can get the power turned on." Even Raleigh was beginning to lose spirit after seeing the layers of dust. A spider had built one terrific web in one corner of the room. "Trash bags should be in the laundry room. Cleaning supplies too. There, or underneath the kitchen sink. The faster we get moving, the quicker we'll be done."

"That's a sight," Randy, her keyboard player, said.

She shot him a warning look.

"What is?" she asked.

"I don't believe I've ever seen you with a broom in your hand before." His face broke into a wide smile. The others laughed. He could always be counted on to break the tension in a room and lighten the mood.

Raleigh laughed too.

"Well, get used to it. You'll probably see me do a whole lot more new things over the next two weeks than you have in fourteen years," she quipped. "I can do a whole lot more than sing."

"Are you threatening to cook again?" Randy teased with a wink. He had a wife, two kids, and a heart of gold. He was an original band member and she looked at him like she would a brother if she'd had siblings.

"I think we all know who caught the bus on fire one time. No use rehashing one little mistake," she shot back before shooing everyone out of the kitchen with her broom.

Raleigh glanced around the room. The place wasn't huge but it was cozy. She'd had countless meals sitting at the table pushed up next to the window. Nana would crack the window so they could hear the birds sing while they ate. Nana could cook. And she didn't stop there. She could bake the most amazing cookies, pies, and cakes.

No, Raleigh hadn't inherited her cooking skills, but she'd been taught how to clean up after herself. She pulled her hair off her face with the rubber band she kept at the ready on her wrist. An hour and forty-five minutes later, the kitchen was spotless and she was finishing scrubbing dust off the original hardwood floors.

"Buck found the generator." Kenny's voice startled her.

She gasped and clutched her chest. She sat back on her heels and blew a loose tendril of hair out of her eyes. "You scared the bejesus out of me, Kenny."

"Sorry." He put his hands up, palms out in the surrender position. "I thought I'd come over and check to see if you needed a hand."

"I'm almost finished. Thanks, though," she said, figuring she had about as much dirt on her as had once been on the floor.

"I'm real sorry about your Nana too," he continued. "Wish I could have been there for you."

"The flowers you and your wife sent were more than enough," she said.

"*Ex*-wife," he corrected.

Raleigh didn't want to go down that road again with him right now. He'd been hinting they should pick up where they'd left off a hundred years ago after she'd overheard his conversation. No thanks. "You know what?"

He cocked a brow.

"You can help me if your offer still stands," she said, needing to stretch her legs.

"Name it." His dimpled smile wouldn't last when he heard what she was about to say.

"Get the wash started with linens. And figure out what to do for dinner. Pizzas maybe?" She pushed up to standing and her knees creaked and groaned. When did she get this old?

His "All right," came after a long pause. He'd been expecting a much different answer, but then again Kenny was used to getting whatever he wanted from the opposite sex.

"Thank you." She pulled off the rubber gloves she'd been wearing and tossed them under the sink in the cleaning supply bucket. "Save me a slice?"

"Where are you headed?" His expression turned sour faster than milk left sitting in the August heat.

"Out," she said as she freed her hair from the rubber band and then pocketed her cell phone. "Don't worry. I know this area like the back of my hand."

Before she could make it out the back door, Hardy walked in the kitchen. "Mind if I join you?"

"You can if you want but I'll be fine going alone. I can't

say for how long though. Once word gets out we're here, you'll have your hands full. But tonight, no one knows I'm back. Not even my more hardcore fans know I'm from Lone Star Pass." She didn't want to tell the man how to do his job. Everything she'd said was true. Sharon had insisted early on they tell everyone Raleigh's hometown was Austin. She didn't have the same last name as Nana, so no one would track Raleigh here. "I have a small window to be on this land undetected, Hardy."

She pinched her thumb and forefinger together.

"And it's shrinking by the minute," she warned. "So, I'm heading out that door. Come if you have to."

Hardy followed her. He stayed back, seeming to know it was a good idea to give her space.

Was her old minibike still in the shed? She made a beeline toward the old building. It had seemed much bigger when she lived here. It struck her as funny how grand everything had seemed to be as a child, and how tiny it seemed now.

In truth, the house was decent size. Though not nearly as large as she'd remembered. The land was still vast, but she was going to need a machete if she wanted to walk around. The sound of a riding lawn mower's engine gave her an idea.

The minibike was right where she'd left it. Albeit the tires needed air. She located the pump and filled them. Had Nana maintained it in the hopes Raleigh would visit more?

Nana had been one of Raleigh's best cheerleaders from the minute she declared she wanted to sing and play guitar for a living. The older woman nearly burst with pride every time they met up in another city. Guilt stabbed Raleigh for being too busy to visit Nana while she was alive. Raleigh would never forgive herself for missing holidays, birthdays, and special occasions, no matter how much Nana reassured it was no big deal. Putting her career above all else got her where she was...but recently she wondered if it was enough.

Raleigh threw her leg over the minibike and started the engine. It had been jerry-rigged a long time ago so she wouldn't need a key since she couldn't seem to hold onto them. She popped a wheelie on her way out of the shed, and then turned right toward the Firebrand Ranch, her second home.

From her sideview mirror, she watched Hardy as he ran, trying to keep up. There was no way he could outrun Red Devil. The minibike was black with spray-painted flames on its sides, but the name was also a nod to her fiery red hair and some might say her temper. She called it passion.

Raleigh shouldn't ride straight to her neighbor's barn. Except she did that very thing, cutting off the engine of Red Devil at the tree line. She squatted as the sun hid behind the mesquite trees, ensuring no one saw her.

This place brought back so many happy memories and she wanted to fly under the radar. Exhausted from the recent event and life on the road in general, she had to remember what she loved about singing in the first place.

She made it into the barn unseen. It was dimly lit inside. She climbed the round metal staircase to the loft where she'd written her first song. She leaned her head against the wooden beam...

And then she heard the door creak open downstairs. Her heart jackhammered her ribs and her pulse pounded. She pocketed her cell and stood against the beam, praying no one would find her up there.

2

Brax Firebrand muttered a curse. This was the second time he'd misplaced his wallet this week. Don't even get him started on his keys. He'd lost count. It was a good thing he lived in the kind of town where keys were normally left inside his truck at all times and belonged to a family well known enough for folks to give him whatever he needed with a signature.

Several of his brothers and cousins had left Firebrand Ranch the minute they'd come of age. Not Brax. Being a Firebrand, living and working the land, was his life.

It did nothing to help with keeping track of his personal belongings though.

The barn was the last place he remembered having his wallet, and he hoped it was still there. Ranch hands could be real comedians when they wanted to be and he didn't want to be on the wrong side of another prank.

Plus, there was a recent crime that had touched the family. Everyone was a little bit on edge since his brother Adam's ex-girlfriend had been murdered, leaving him with an infant daughter he never knew existed.

The barn was as good a place as any to begin the search. Eyes to the floor, there was an open space when he first entered followed by a string of small offices to his left. A row of stables sat to his right. The tack room was around the stables and to the right.

There was a loft upstairs that...

A piece of hay drifting down like a feather caught his eye. No one should be in the barn at this hour. If someone was in the loft, Brax needed to give himself an advantage. Anyone who knew him would have called out the minute the barn door opened, which meant the person who was up there didn't want to be noticed. He walked over to the light switch and dimmed the lights until he could barely see his hand in front of his face. His wallet must have fallen out of his back pocket because he found it next to the stairs.

An eerie feeling settled over him after recent events. The murderer had been caught but a horrific crime in his own backyard wasn't something he could erase from his thoughts so easily.

Brax moved to the metal staircase. He toed off his boots so he could slip up quietly in his socks, a trick he'd learned having eight brothers and nine cousins around, all boys no less. They'd explored and memorized every inch of the barn and much of the land as well, especially anything close to the main house.

With the stealth of a lion closing in on its prey, Brax made progress toward his target. His eyes weren't adjusted to the dark, but he didn't have time to waste.

At some point, it occurred to him the prowler he was stalking might actually be a barn cat. Still, he was on edge and taking nothing for granted after recent events.

A noise to his right drew his attention. Something small had been tossed...an acorn?

He immediately spun left and grabbed the shadow beside him. Before it could register this person was much smaller than him and smelled a whole helluva lot better, he had her back against the wall and his hands pinning her there.

"It's Raleigh," the shaky voice said.

"Prove it." He would have known if Raleigh was back in town. His brother had convinced him to go to Austin a time or two to hear her sing but there was no way she was back. She'd be news now that she was a big deal.

"I swear," she said, and he recognized her voice this time. "Raleigh Perry," she continued, irritation laced her voice. There was no fear in her tone now. She was all ire and attitude. "Now, let me go and I'll prove it."

He one-armed her to hold her in place, not completely convinced she was the real deal. He fished his cell out of his pocket and with a flick of his thumb, the flashlight app brightened the darkness. He shined it at her and she immediately squinted and turned her face away.

"What the heck, Brax?" she managed to say.

He let go of her and she issued a sharp sigh.

"You scared me to death. What's wrong with you?" she said as her chest heaved.

"Well, I didn't mean to but I wasn't exactly expecting anyone to be hiding in the loft, and we've had trouble in town recently. Let's go downstairs and turn on the light so we can see each other when we talk." He led the way, unsure if she would follow. The one thing he remembered about Raleigh was that she was headstrong.

He walked over to the switch and flipped the light on. She sat on the bottom step, twiddling a piece of hay in between her fingers.

"Hey, I didn't mean to trespass," she started but he waved

her off, still in slight disbelief the famous singer was in the barn.

"Come on, it's not a big deal," he said. "You surprised me is all. Plus, I feel like the last time I saw you here, you were like," he held his hand three feet off the floor, "this tall."

Raleigh's cheeks turned a few shades of red and he couldn't help but notice that she had grown into a beautiful woman. Although beautiful seemed too generic a term for her. Her long red hair framed an oval face with the creamiest skin dotted with freckles. She resembled a famous redheaded TV star who had a popular show, a show his mother was addicted to. She'd have it on in the kitchen while cooking. And then there was her body with those long runner's legs of hers. Don't even get him started on her voice, which was smooth as silk.

She recovered when she said, "There was a bomb threat at my last concert. Turned out to be real."

"That's wild and scary as hell," he said, realizing it must be the reason she was hiding in his family's barn. This had been a second home to her growing up. She was four years younger than him. They'd gotten along about as well as a sister and brother could. If those siblings fought over every little thing. But there was nothing sisterly about the way she was making his heart batter his ribcage. He chalked it up to being surprised. "They caught him, right?"

"Nope." She cupped her face in her hands. Then, she looked up and he had an unexpected reaction when their eyes met. A jolt of electricity rocketed through him. He had to remind himself this was little Raleigh. Only his body pointed out the fact she'd grown up. Suddenly the four years between them didn't seem so shocking.

"Sounds like a mess," he admitted.

"It is," she said with more than a hint of fear and stress in her voice.

"I'm guessing the law is involved," he said.

She nodded.

"They must have some idea who would do this. Leads?" He chalked his level of concern up to their shared history, and not the way she seemed to stir his heart.

"None so far. The threat was called in and, of course, we all thought it was a hoax. These things usually are," she said like it was another day at the office.

"How often do you deal with threats?" He couldn't wrap his mind around how awful that must be.

"It's not too bad. Every once in a while you get a fan who's a little too into me, but you just keep moving forward, you know?" She said the words like he would have an idea what it was like to be a singing sensation.

He threw his hands up and shrugged.

"I deal with poachers and the bad ones can be pretty dangerous. But I know what I'm dealing with and they're on my turf," he said. "I can't imagine being on stage and looking out onto a crowd of strangers wondering who might have rigged a bomb underneath."

"It's not the best part about my job. Honestly, I can't let it get inside my head or it would be game over. And there is so much I love about what I do," she said. "Besides, as soon as the threat came through, we postponed my performances."

"From what my mom says, you've made it. Bona fide country star." His mother had been following Raleigh's career ever since she left Lone Star Pass for Austin at eighteen.

Raleigh laughed and it was nice to see her smile. Her face lit up and a dozen campfires lit inside him at the sight.

"I wouldn't say that exactly," she quickly countered.

"Your fans say otherwise," he said.

"I'm a Regional Wonder at best." She laughed at her own joke and he couldn't help but do the same. "Remind me not to tell you what that means later."

"How long until its safe for you to get back on the road?" His mother would want to know all the details.

"We've canceled the next two weeks' worth of shows, so we'll see after that. This guy seems like the real deal. We have to give the feds time to track him down and arrest him. Get him off the streets," she said. "He threatened me in particular."

"Jerk," he spit out. His protective instincts kicked into overdrive. This was Raleigh. They'd practically grown up under the same roof. It was natural for him to be enraged at the thought someone wanted to hurt her and not because he felt a pull of attraction toward her stronger than anything he'd ever experienced.

"My sentiments exactly."

RALEIGH HAD BEEN CAUGHT off guard by Brax finding her. But it was good to see him despite the fact he'd annoyed her more than the others growing up, teasing her about her pigtails and freckles.

"Hey, I'm sorry to hear all this. You've worked hard for your success and some random jerk shouldn't have the ability to take it away from you even for a few weeks." Brax's voice washed over her like Amaretto over vanilla ice cream.

She performed another mental headshake.

This was Brax Firebrand. The guy who'd teased and tormented her mercilessly growing up, when he bothered to notice her at all.

She crossed her legs and folded her arms. "You were a real brat when we were kids. You know that, right?"

He laughed.

"Yeah? So were you if memory serves. What did we use to call you?" He seemed to be searching his mind. "Oh, right the Red Streak."

"I almost blocked that name completely from my thoughts," she said with a chuckle. "But Red Devil seemed to be your personal favorite."

"You had that minibike." He snapped his fingers a couple of times. "You would steal my bandana and take off on that thing. You were such a squirt."

"Me? You guys weren't any better if memory serves." Pretending to be offended didn't last long. She broke into a smile. "Yeah, I was rotten when I wanted to be."

"Resilient might be a better word," he admitted. "Looking back, it couldn't have been easy to be dumped into a world of eighteen boys."

"Made me strong," she mused. There was a whole lot of truth to that statement. Besides, the Firebrand boys, now men she noted, were respectable people. Not one got into serious trouble with school. Hardworking with a whole lot of testosterone; they were bound to bump heads based on the sheer number of them all living on one property.

"That's one way to look at it." Brax Firebrand was six-feet-one-inch of male hotness. His hair could best be described as dirty brown against eyes so blue they popped. Even as a teenager, he'd been shorter than the others and she'd overheard his cousins teasing him that he was the runt of the family. The other side of the Firebrand family could be real jerks when they wanted to be.

Raleigh blushed looking at the man he'd become. No runt here. He'd always been good-looking in that rugged outdoorsy way. Most of the time he'd had on a cowboy hat but she still remembered those honest blue eyes.

Then, there were his arms. A person shouldn't have so many stacked muscles in one place. Butterflies got loose in her stomach just thinking about his touch when he'd pinned her up against the wall earlier.

This seemed like a good time to remind herself that Brax Firebrand had been a royal pain growing up. He'd always been quick tempered, as well as quick to make up his mind about something. The word obstinate came to mind. So did bull-headed.

"Being back here must seem small-time compared to being on the road." He interrupted her thoughts, his voice sliding over her, causing her arms to goose bump.

She cleared her throat to ease the dryness. Brax should not be making her mouth feel like she'd just licked a glue stick. Was it getting hot in the barn?

"Are you kidding? Being here is everything." She heard her own voice crack.

He shot her a confused look.

"I love my career, don't get me wrong. But this feels like home." She looked around the barn thinking how it seemed smaller too. Cozy. "Did you know it all started here?"

"Wait a minute. Here? I had no idea. How is that even possible?" He quirked a brow and it was dangerously sexy.

Seriously?

"I wrote my first song up there." She nodded toward the loft.

"That's news to me," he admitted.

"Because I can count on one hand how many people know that particular piece of information." She held up two fingers, one for him and one for her. She wasn't sure why she felt the need to share, except being home caused her to relax. She didn't realize how tense she'd become on the road even before the bomb situation.

"Who is the lucky second?" he asked with a damn sparkle in his eyes that made her want to stare at him for days.

"That would be me."

"Well then, I'm honored." He stood up straighter and his voice changed.

"Do me a favor," she said.

"Depends on what it is," he countered.

"Just treat me like you used to. Like nothing's changed." She felt her shoulders deflate a little when she said the words.

"You got it, Red Streak," he teased.

Brax could be real annoying when he wanted to be.

"Good. Thanks," she said with a smile. She might not love that nickname but it sure was nice to see Brax.

"Can I ask a question?" He stood there, arms over his chest.

"Shoot," she said.

"Why do you call Austin home?" he asked. "I got the impression you were embarrassed about being from such a small town."

"Nope." She responded without hesitation, catching his gaze. "Some things are sacred, you know? You just don't want to share them with the world. Plus, I always wanted to protect Nana and her piece of serenity here. Since I have my dad's last name, we don't...didn't match. She could fly under the radar without having reporters or groupies hanging out on her fence, trying to find out what I was like when I was a young girl or if I was about to come home for a visit."

"Explains why no one's ever connected you to the town," he said after a thoughtful pause. He smiled, like he approved of the decision. For some reason, that small smile made her heart leap with joy. *What the heck?* She chalked it up to being happy to be home, and back at the barn, and not the fact that being here with Brax had her pulse pounding.

"Least I could do," she said.

"It was nice of you to protect your nana," he continued. "I don't believe I've ever seen someone as proud as she was." He lowered his head for a few seconds before looking up and catching her gaze. "I was sorry to hear of her passing."

"Thank you, Brax." That frog in her throat feeling returned.

"Work must have kept you on the road during..."

His voice trailed off but she knew what he was going to say next.

"You were at her funeral?" She wasn't sure why she was so shocked. His mother was a dear friend of Nana's and it would make sense her sons would attend.

"Of course," was all he said.

"I was too," she admitted. "But, I had a concert that night in Houston I couldn't miss. I kept a low profile at the service."

"Sorry I missed you. I would have offered my condolences in person," he said.

"I appreciate the thought, Brax." She couldn't look away despite the twinge of guilt trying to gnaw at her insides for not sticking around that day. "Keeping busy is good for grief."

He nodded like he had personal knowledge of the fact.

"Everyone here okay?" she asked.

"The Marshall passed away at the end of last month." He shook his head.

"I'm so sorry, Brax." The Marshall kept everyone at arm's length according to her memory, but the Firebrands were a tight-knit bunch. Losing the patriarch of the family would be hard on them all.

"It's only been a couple of weeks and the fighting has already begun," Brax admitted.

"Your dad and uncle have never gotten along." She remembered there being a clear division amongst the two sides. Shame, she thought, because having a big family sure would be nice after growing up an only child.

"Strange for a pair of brothers to do nothing but argue," he said.

"No offense to the Marshall, but that seemed to be the way he liked it," she admitted.

"True." He didn't argue. The way he tilted his head to the right meant he was thinking hard. "I didn't realize you noticed those things, but I shouldn't be surprised. There were plenty of times I caught you sitting in a quiet corner while taking in the whole scene. My family comes with a lot of moving parts. We were a handful running around the house the way we did, but you'd be at the kitchen table soaking it all in."

"My first manager said that's what makes me a good song writer." She wasn't sure why she was sharing so much, except it felt good to be with Brax, to be home. Of course, she couldn't afford to get too used to the feeling considering she'd be back on the road soon enough. Leaving Lone Star Pass never got any easier and she had a feeling it was about to get a whole lot worse.

Raleigh stood up, needing some distance, some space from this old friend who evoked so much emotion in her. "I should get back to Nana...*my* place." She issued a sharp sigh. "I don't think I'll ever get used to saying those words."

"It sure has been good seeing you, Raleigh," he said, and

her chest squeezed. He was being polite. Why did she wish he'd ask her to stay instead?

She chalked it up to being homesick and walked right past him with a nod. Halfway out the door, she paused.

"Stop by tomorrow if you want. Meet the band," she said.

"I have work to do. Thanks, though."

"No problem. The offer stands for you and any of your family." She added the last part on a whim. And then she realized what she'd done. "On second thought. We're trying to stay under the radar. Do you mind if you keep running into me between us?"

He held up two fingers.

"Just us," he said with a masculine voice that traveled all over her. Her traitorous heart leapt again as she canceled the thought she was going to regret walking out the door. Would she though?

3

Hardy stood at the back door as Raleigh walked up and Jake sat on the steps. It was dark. She'd ditched him earlier and the look on his face told her exactly how upset he was about her antics. Jake's face twisted with concern. He didn't even bother to speak to her. He pushed to standing and circled around toward the front of the house.

"My bad." She put her hands in the air to show surrender to Hardy.

"I can't do my job if you split off like that," he warned. He was a tank of a man who would intimidate most folks. Precisely the reason he'd been hired for the tour.

"You're right. I'm sorry." She hated the thought of being in her hometown and under twenty-four seven supervision, but she'd hired him to do a job and she needed to let him do it. "I won't pull another stunt like that again."

Hardy took a step back to allow her passage, but he gave her the death stare she probably deserved as she passed by. To be fair, there was plenty of security on the Firebrand property. Of course, she knew how to get around it, but most folks didn't, and Hardy knew nothing of it either way.

News would get out that she was in town soon enough and it wouldn't be safe for her to step outside. She hated the thought of being imprisoned on Nana's property and those few precious hours stolen at the barn would have to be enough to get her through this rough patch.

"Pizza is in the fridge," Hardy begrudgingly said.

"Thanks," was all she said before she grabbed a couple of cold slices and then placed them on top of a paper towel.

Kenny casually walked into the room wearing only his boxers. The man worked out and had nice, olive skin, but they had rules about being dressed in mixed company.

"Hey, foul," she said to him.

"I didn't think it was a big deal since you were gone," he countered with a raised eyebrow and a shaming tone of voice. The man had nerve. She would give him that.

"I'm here now," she said. "You know the rules."

"I won't forget next time," he promised with a smile that made his dimple wink at her.

Come on. Did he think that was all he had to do to smooth things over?

"Good. You still owe a hundred dollars." The 'rule violation' jar was on the tour bus. She clearly needed to bring it inside and keep it visible. She'd grab it tomorrow. All she could think about tonight was food, shower, bed.

The pizza didn't make it to her old bedroom. Everything was as she'd left it, like it was stuck in a time capsule from when she'd been eighteen. There was a bed, nightstand with a lamp, and a desk for homework. Everything had been cleaned off and boxed up before she took off on her first tour, except for a few framed photos of her and Nana. Then there was Raleigh's best friend who'd gone off to college and down a career, marriage, and family track. The two had lost touch despite believing they'd be friends forever during high school.

As she grabbed pajamas and her robe, Kenny came strolling in the room.

"What are you doing in here?" she asked.

"We have to double up on rooms. Three bedrooms for eight people. Buck is sleeping on the tour bus along with Jake. That leaves you and me." His smirk was infuriating.

"No dice, buddy," she countered. "One of us is sleeping on the couch downstairs or on the bus with Buck and Jake, and I don't care which one of us it is."

Tim walked out of Nana's room and stopped in front of the doorway. "There a problem?"

"As a matter of fact, there is. No sleeping with mixed company. Remember the rule?" she asked Kenny.

"Only on tour. Technically, this doesn't count," Kenny immediately countered.

"Looks like I'll be the one sleeping on the couch then." There was no way she planned to share a room with Kenny.

"That doesn't seem right," Tim said. "Me and Willie can take our beds on the bus. You stay in your grandmother's room."

"I don't want to—"

"It's settled," Tim cut in. "We don't mind. We're used to sleeping in there and at least it won't be moving this time."

He shot a look at Kenny that could have caught ice on fire. She shouldn't get as much satisfaction out of it as she did.

"Thank you for being a gentleman," she said to Tim.

"There's only a twin bed in here. It makes more sense for me to sleep on the bus than uproot the two of you," Kenny relented.

She wasn't sure what he thought he was going to win by forcing the issue of being a couple with her. Or, maybe he thought she wouldn't be able to resist him shirtless. She almost laughed out loud.

The man had a great bod. She would give him that. But there was so much more to a relationship than a pretty outer shell. A little voice in the back of her mind picked that moment to point out Brax Firebrand had it all.

"It's settled then," she said, looking first to Tim and then to Kenny.

Both nodded.

"Next time, we should probably make arrangements together as a group," she said.

"We would have if you'd been here," Kenny said low and under his breath.

Rather than turn around and tell him off, she bit down on her temper and headed to the bathroom instead. A nice shower was all she needed to wash the day away. Of course, that annoying voice said she should have stayed in the barn with Brax longer.

The shower was just what the doctor ordered. She closed the door to her bedroom when she'd finished, thankful for a little privacy. It was a rare thing being on the road with seven guys at all times, sometimes eight when Wade showed up. She retrieved her laptop from her bag. She imagined it had been Kenny who'd been 'kind' enough to bring her suitcase upstairs and into the room he thought they would be sharing. She shook off her frustration, figuring she had enough on her mind without dealing with him.

She opened her laptop, powered up, and climbed onto her bed. Someone had washed the blanket. She owed them a thank-you come morning. Either the generator was doing its job or they'd tripped a breaker instead of losing all power. The latter was most likely considering it used to happen all the time with the old house.

Wade would have phoned if a suspect was in custody, but she googled the incident anyway. Seeing the images of the venue roped off behind 'crime scene' tape and people held behind barricades sent a shiver racing down her spine. The thought of being some obsessed person's target sent another.

Looking at these images much longer and sleep would be impossible. Raleigh opened her e-mail instead. Wade was supposed to e-mail her financial statements for the past six months. Did he? No.

She glanced at the clock. Was it too late to call him? Probably. She sent a text instead, asking when he planned to join them.

No response came.

She would try again at first light. It was getting late and she should probably shut down for the night. A couple of minutes later, she was tucked under her covers, looking out the same window she had when she'd dreamed of being a country singer.

Dreams really did come true. She loved her job. She loved meeting fans. Most of all, she loved making music and sharing it with her small corner of the world. She might not be 'world tour' big, but she had a nice following and got to do the music she wanted to with people who were like family at this point. Kenny had always marched to his own drummer. He'd get the hint at some point and their friendship could get back on track. For now, she planned to keep him at arm's length until he moved on to someone else. And he would. Kenny wasn't the type to stay single for long.

Her thoughts drifted to Brax. If she was going to be in a

relationship with someone, she'd want it to be with someone like him. Well someone like him who was a little less annoying.

BRAX PUNCHED HIS PILLOW. He rolled onto his left side. Then, his right. For reasons he didn't want to examine, he was concerned about Raleigh's life. He tried to chalk his restlessness up to the fact he knew her on a personal level, but it ran deeper. He tried to convince himself she was like a sister but that couldn't be further from the truth. Not even when his mother used to babysit her when they were younger did he ever look at her in that light.

Why couldn't he stop thinking about her?

Four a.m. couldn't get there fast enough. At three-thirty, he gave up trying to sleep in favor of a morning workout and shower. He decided to head to the barn early to see if anyone was there.

He struck out there too. There were lights on in the main house so he figured he'd check on his brother Adam and his new family. Adam was recovering from being stabbed during an altercation with an attorney who'd been fixated on Adam's daughter Angel. His brother was recovering and probably needed a hand while healing despite having found the love of his life, a woman by the name of Prudence. Plus, the coffee was better there.

Brax slipped in through the backdoor and immediately heard voices in the kitchen. He recognized Adam's and their mother's immediately. It made sense for their mother to be at Adam's new place considering she had a long history of jumping at the chance to babysit girls and now officially had a granddaughter.

"That's not important," his mother said in her defensive tone.

"What's not?" Brax asked from behind her, figuring Adam needed an assist. Their mother was one of the most caring and loving people on the planet. She had a heart of gold but was born stubborn as an ox.

Their mother gasped and brought her hand up to cover her mouth the minute she turned and saw him. Her cheeks turned several shades of red, like she'd been caught with her hand in the cookie jar.

"Nothing," she said a little too quickly.

"I'm trying to get our mother to explain to me why she knows someone who can doctor a birth certificate," Adam said plain as day.

"What on earth?" Brax asked, completely thrown off guard.

"I was merely suggesting that I might be able to help." She threw her hands up in the air and sucked in a breath. More moves he'd seen her pull when she was guilty of something. But what?

The woman was practically a saint. Anyone in town would agree except maybe their aunt but she was a piece of work. Their mother brought up her own sons with very little outside help while caring for her friends' children when needed. She was the first to volunteer if there was a committee for park cleanup or a toy drive for underprivileged kids. She managed this side of the family's charitable contributions and their father had groaned more than once about her generosity.

"With her network of friends, I guess I'm not as surprised as I probably should be," Brax quipped. He pointed toward the coffee maker and got a nod of approval from Adam. "You want a cup?"

"I'll take a refill," Adam picked up his mug and stood. He winced, froze, and then looked like he was trying to shake off the pain. "I don't care how much it hurts, I'm not taking any more of those pain meds. They make me dizzy and nauseous, not a great combination. I knew I should have stuck with two ibuprofen and called it a day."

"Eat something and drink some milk to coat your stomach," their mom said. She was already on her way to the fridge.

"It won't do any good to argue," Brax said to his brother as Adam started to protest.

Adam laughed instead.

"There isn't an animal alive more stubborn than our mother," Adam said. He sat back down, accepting his fate.

Brax grabbed his brother's mug, refilled it and had it back in two shakes. He took a sip of coffee and waited for the burn to kick in.

Their mother was suddenly so interested in whatever was in the fridge she started humming. Was it an act? What was she covering up? "This looks good in here. It's well stocked. I asked your grandfather's housekeeper to continue to bring food for you and Prudence. You are injured and both of you are caring for my beautiful granddaughter."

"Did you notice how quickly she just changed the subject?" Brax whispered to Adam.

"I sure did. She acts suspicious every time I bring it up now," Adam admitted.

"But what? How?" Brax couldn't fathom her being dishonest. "She's like the original Girl Scout. She couldn't possibly be involved in anything illegal, let alone immoral. Maybe you misunderstood."

"You know what she said to me when she mentioned she

had a guy who could alter Angel's birth certificate?" Adam asked but his question was rhetorical.

Brax shook his head.

"Something along the lines of, 'parents do what they have to in order to protect their children.'" Adam shot a look before taking a sip of coffee.

"That sort of sounds exactly like her in a strange way." Brax tried to justify her statement. She was the type of mother who would do literally anything for her children. And yet, she was also one of the most honest people he knew. So, yeah, that statement was a little confusing.

"You're missing the point, though," Adam said.

"And that is?"

"Why would *she* have to make a choice like that?" Adam was spot on.

"Only our mother can answer that question," Brax stated. There was a niggling feeling at the back of his mind. He wanted to tell Adam that Raleigh was in town, especially as Adam had dragged Brax to Austin to hear her sing more than once over the years.

"How about huevos rancheros?" Mother announced.

"Anything sounds good to me. I don't usually eat more than toast," Brax said.

"So, Mom, you never did answer the question," Adam continued. He was on the trail like a bloodhound following a scent.

Mother almost dropped the skillet. Panic darkened her brown eyes as she fumbled to place it on the countertop. "I hear the baby. I'm just going to run up and see if Prudence needs my help."

She scattered out of the room faster than a flock of birds following a gunshot.

"See what I mean?" Adam asked. He set his coffee cup

down on the oversized wooden table. "There's no way she could hear the baby from all the way down here."

Adam, Prudence, and the baby had taken up residence in the east wing of the main house. He was right. There was no baby monitor in the kitchen. Sound wouldn't travel from the upstairs bedroom to here.

"What does she have to act suspicious about?" Now, Brax was intrigued.

4

Raleigh woke with the sun. She stretched her arms out and sat up. Being in her childhood home, in her old bed, gave her the best night of sleep she'd had in a long time.

A racket outside drew her to the window. She pulled back the curtain to find a gaggle of young people being forced to stay off the property by Hardy.

They'd found her. Was it the tour bus? She'd purposely kept hers low-key. The one with all the lights had her face and name running down both sides, and that was the one fans followed after a concert, thinking she was inside, instead of the nondescript bus parked next to it. The decoy worked.

Of course, she thought, people knew her here. Folks were proud of her and had supported her career. She should have realized they'd know it was her once the tour bus pulled into Nana's place. These folks knew who she really was.

That meant reporters might soon follow.

Raleigh heaved a sigh. Her stomach growled. A good

night of sleep did wonders for her stress levels. But her stomach reminded her that she hadn't eaten since last night's cold pizza.

It didn't take but ten minutes to throw on clothes and freshen up. She ran a brush through her hair. It was still ironed out, and had held its shape. She grabbed a jar of tinted lip gloss, figuring a natural pink would brighten her face, in case someone snapped a shot of her.

The middle of June called for jeans and a summer shirt.

Someone had brought in muffins last night. She grabbed a blueberry one and popped it inside the clean microwave that she'd scrubbed herself. There was a sense of pride that came with the small accomplishment. She rarely had time for anything but concerts, band meetings, and making new music. Other basics had to take a backseat. Basics like cooking and cleaning up her own kitchen. The most she did on tour was heat something in the microwave in a plastic dish, then throw away the disposable container when she was done.

It was crazy how satisfying attending to the little things could be.

Raleigh polished off the muffin and downed a quick cup of coffee. Thinking about running into Brax at the barn last night caused her cheeks to heat and that butterfly sensation to return to her stomach. She must be losing her damn mind.

Before she could go too far down that road, she grabbed sunglasses and slipped out the back door before anyone realized she was awake. Once she got to the Firebrands, she would text Hardy to let him know she was okay. He wouldn't expect her up for a few more hours though. And he was currently preoccupied with trying to keep the small crowd that was forming off her property line.

The shed was unlocked, so she walked right in. This time, she grabbed her old helmet off the nail and then placed it over her head. That should help keep her identity under wraps. She pushed the minibike into the woods, not wanting to draw attention from the crowd out front or from her bandmates.

Jake, who was usually the sweetest and most innocent one of the group, had been upset by her leaving last night without taking anyone with her for protection. She hadn't seen him yet this morning to know if he'd gotten over it. The kid normally treated her like she walked on water, all starry-eyed. She hated to burst his bubble, but she was a normal person just like everyone else, she just happened to have a career in the spotlight.

Once she was out of earshot, she threw her leg over the seat and then started the engine. Being on Red Devil made her smile. The wind whipped against her as she navigated around the trees, up and down small hills and around the creek.

Don't get her wrong, she loved what she did for a living but it came with a price, and that was personal freedom.

Just as the Firebrand property line came into view, she heard the roar of an ATV gunning toward her. The male rider wasn't wearing a helmet. She didn't recognize him as local but to be fair, it had been a long time since she'd lived in Lone Star Pass.

And yet, the way he stared at her with those determined eyes sent her pulse racing. A burst of adrenaline caused her hands to tremble as she twisted the throttle with her right hand.

It didn't matter who this guy was, she planned to let him eat her dust.

Normally, she had to get off her minibike in order to

squeeze it through the break in fencing but with the ATV closing in, there was no time. She cut left, drawing him away from the property. If she could get enough of a lead, she could lose this guy and double back.

An icy chill raced down her back at the thought that he might be the bomber who seemed intent on taking her out. To what end?

He could silence her. Then what? What would he have to gain? Then again, she'd read about worse things happening to good folks for no reason other than someone snapped and decided to take out as many folks as he could. Her threat had been targeted, directed at her. The thought sent an icy chill racing down her back.

She cut right again, and the ATV followed right along. This situation was going from bad to worse as he was cutting her off from going back to her house. She tried not to think about how stupid she'd been for putting herself at risk by going out by herself. It would serve her right if something happened...

And yet she couldn't go there.

His ATV was faring better with the terrain they were on. He had more stability with four tires and these little hills were perfect for him. She had to take it easy or risk getting too much air, giving him an unfair advantage. To make matters worse, she wasn't rocking a big engine with her minibike.

Think. Think. Think.

That was it. She needed to outthink him. She knew the area. Did he?

There was only one way to find out.

A flat area would give her the speed advantage. The meadow wasn't too far away. She was also nimbler than the ATV. So, she started cutting her turns faster and then speeding up whenever she had some clearing. The path along the creek would give her flat ground.

It was closer than the meadow and he was gaining on her again.

Leaning left, she made a hard turn toward the creek and then twisted the throttle as far as it would go. She risked a glance back and was rewarded with a tree stump in the way. A sharp turn wasn't enough to avoid contact. Her front tire nicked the tree stump and she felt herself go flying.

A yelp escaped before she could rein it in. Her head landed a foot away from the base of a large oak. She'd been thrown a good five feet and for a split-second waited for the pain of a broken bone to strike.

When none came, she scrambled up onto all fours and recited a gratitude prayer Nana had taught her when she wasn't much bigger than a fly.

The problem was that her engine ku-klunked and then died. Out of gas?

The ATV driver sneered as he aimed directly toward her. She stood up and glanced around. Could she run? Climb a tree?

Since she'd never made a good squirrel, she went for option number one. She threw off her helmet to minimize any extra weight that might slow her down, and ran.

The ATV engine roared. He was letting her know that he was coming for her. She could almost see the smirk on his face. Since rolling over and giving up wasn't in her DNA, she ran harder. Branches slapped at her as she headed into a thicket. He'd never get his ATV through the trees ahead if she could beat him there.

Of course, a foot chase might be a different story and she couldn't risk a glance back to see if he was gaining on her.

And then out of nowhere, the ATV engine faded. The

rider was still on the thing because the engine buzzed. Her mind snapped to the fear of a black bear being out here. Or wild hog. Those could really butcher a person. Either one would stop the ATV in his tracks.

Heart hammering her ribcage, she risked a glance to see what had caused the jerk to split.

The answer was immediate. Brax Firebrand stood there. His back was to her, but his stance said he was aiming a pistol at the ATV driver. Thank the stars for small miracles.

Raleigh called out to Brax, figuring it best not to surprise a man with his finger already on the trigger.

BRAX TURNED his head toward the sound of Raleigh's voice, keeping the barrel of his pistol aimed at the trespassing jerk. He'd heard her yelp and knew she was in trouble. A little piece of his heart wanted her to be coming back to see him. He shut that down before it could take hold.

The ATV driver turned tail, and for a split second, Brax thought about going after the guy. The move would leave Raleigh alone and vulnerable. Brax wouldn't risk it.

"Your timing is perfect. I'm not sure what I would have done if you hadn't intervened." The words came out through gasps. Raleigh bent forward like she was struggling to catch her breath.

"I thought I heard Red Devil out here. Came over to investigate." Relief washed over him at making it in time.

"You saved my backside, and it's very much appreciated." She stood up, and pinched her side with her freehand. "I am way more out of shape than I realized. You'd think with all those concerts I'd be in better form."

"How much running do you do on stage?" His question was rhetorical.

"True. Mental note...add a cardio workout to my morning stretches," she said, the fear in her eyes belied her casual remarks. She'd always been tough on the outside.

"Any idea who that was?" He motioned toward the direction the ATV driver had disappeared. There was no sign of him or sound of a motor but that didn't mean he was gone. Brax surveyed the area, ignoring the way his pulse kicked up a few notches every time Raleigh was near.

"None," she admitted. "And the only description I got would probably match half of Lone Star Pass.

"Then we should probably get out of here before he circles back," Brax said. "I scared him away for the moment. Doesn't mean he won't regroup and come at us again."

She nodded.

"Any chance you have any gasoline on you?" Her perusal shouldn't kick up his pulse another notch. And yet, it did.

He tucked the pistol in its holster and shook his head.

"Have a horse tied up that way." He motioned toward the property line. "I can get you to safety and we can deal with the minibike later. Deal?"

She looked like she was contemplating her options even though she had none that he could see. She was also covering the fact her body was trembling ever so slightly, most likely from a mix of adrenaline and fear. Raleigh was clearly rattled by the near encounter with the ATV driver. The very real thought they might have been up close and personal with the bomber raised Brax's blood pressure a few notches.

"Let's go." She retrieved her helmet before walking over to her minibike. She tucked the helmet under the handlebars. "That should keep it safe until we can come back for it."

"After you." He held the fence apart so she could squeeze through before one-arming the post and hopping over. "Bullet is tied up over here."

Brax walked Raleigh to his American Paint Horse. She was well-versed in riding so he didn't have to worry about showing her the ropes. She tucked her left boot in the stirrup, grabbed the horn and saddle, and then threw her right leg up and over in one smooth transaction. He ignored the jolt of electricity that came with contact when he hopped up and on the horse behind her.

She handed over the reins. Bullet gave them a smooth ride back to the barn.

"We can ride back in my pickup so we can bring gasoline." There was always gasoline on hand in the equipment room, never in the barn.

"While we're here, is there any chance I can swing by and see your mother?" Raleigh asked.

"She would like that a lot actually," he said. "I thought you were trying to fly under the radar for as long as possible." He stopped right there when he caught onto the implication and put two-and-two together. "You've been found."

"Woke up to a throng of people outside the front gate. I skipped out on my security detail while he kept them from stampeding the house. Who I need to text before he realizes I'm gone, but I need a few minutes to catch my breath first."

"The attention ever get to you?" The invasion of privacy would drive him crazy.

"Hard to complain when I set myself up for this, you know?" She smiled but it didn't reach her eyes, and he wondered if she refused to let herself feel any differently.

"Still. You're a human being. And a private one at that if

memory serves." He remembered all the times he ran past her while she was picking on the guitar in a quiet corner. She had a streak that had her riding minibikes and racing through his family home. Most of the time, though, she could be found writing in a notebook or strumming the guitar. Once she left Lone Star Pass for the Austin music scene, it all clicked and made sense. The showman in her was getting used to the attention. The songwriter in her sat and observed, then scribbled her thoughts. The musician in her turned them into hits.

"Sometimes," she said and her cheeks flushed. "I didn't think you'd ever noticed me unless I was on Red Devil."

"I didn't," he said. Then, felt the need to clarify. "Not back then anyway."

He hadn't meant to say the last word and her eyes gave away the fact she'd noticed. His throat felt drier than the clay soil during a drought. The current one was about to enter its third year, much to everyone's disappointment. They needed rain.

Before she could say anything, he added, "Mom has been at the main house with Adam's new bride and baby."

"Adam is married? He has a baby? When did that happen?" Her eyes widened in shock. "Hold that thought. Of course, he's married. Some of the others probably are too." She glanced down at his wedding finger and could have sworn he saw relief wash over her when she didn't see a gold band.

"Everyone is single now except for Adam," he said, figuring he didn't need to go into everyone's complicated lives.

She seemed to catch onto the word, *now,* when she gave a knowing look.

"It's strange how I half expected everyone to be exactly

the same as when I left. The same age and at the same place in life…funny how that works because obviously time stands still for no one," she said, her gaze unfocused like she was looking inside herself for the insight. "And maybe it's true that you can never go back once you leave."

"This is my home, so I never had my sights on living anywhere else," he said.

"Yeah," she said. "If I had a cattle ranch legacy, I might have stuck around too," she said with a spark in her eye. It was the look she got when she was headed for mischief.

"Ready to head to the main house?" He wanted to circle back to speak to his mother after she'd ducked out of their questions this morning. He never thought he'd see the day when he heard himself say that his mother was hiding something. Now, he needed to find out what it was and why.

5

"Before we go inside, I should go ahead and let Hardy know where I am. He was already so frustrated with me last night he barely spoke to me, and I'm not going to make it any better if he realizes I'm gone without saying a word again." Raleigh fished her cell out of her back pocket and held it up for Brax to see.

"You want me to head inside?" Brax asked.

"I'd feel better if you stayed out here to be honest," she said. Her response seemed to catch him off guard. But then, he didn't have to worry about a bomber targeting him. Out here, he didn't have to worry about much at all. Poachers came to mind. Raleigh sighed. She wasn't exactly being fair. The Firebrand Ranch just seemed so idyllic and untouchable it was easy to get lulled into a sense of security here. The feeling was half the attraction of coming here. That, and the fact Mrs. Firebrand had treated Raleigh like one of her children. Maybe a little more special at times, since she was a visitor.

Raleigh's third hit had been a tribute to Brax's mom. Funny, she'd never circled back to tell anyone, least of all

Lucia Firebrand. Life had been a whirlwind in those early years. Still was, if she was being honest.

She stared at the cell, thinking she should call Hardy so he could hear her voice and know that she was fine. He didn't know about the ATV, though. Would he be worried?

Either way, he wasn't going to be thrilled with her for leaving the property without giving him a proper heads-up.

With a sharp sigh, she tapped his name on the screen.

Hardy picked up on the first ring.

"I'm sorry," he immediately said. "Where are you?"

She wasn't sure why he was sorry...then it dawned on her something must have happened at the house.

"I'd rather not say in case someone is listening. Suffice it to say that I'm fine," she said.

"There were too many of them," he said and his voice sounded defeated. "They came at us from all directions. I'm just relieved you got out before they breached the house."

"Everyone else get out?" she asked, her pulse kicking up a few notches.

"The mob turned out to be harmless, but you couldn't have known that when they broke through the line," he said. "The guys are all fine and accounted for. We've been worried sick about you though."

Broke through the line?

"Is the house okay?" she asked.

"Things got a little out of hand, but I was able to get everyone under control. There were some superfans in there who got a little too worked up at the thought of seeing you in the flesh," he said. "House is good. I don't want you to come back until we've cleared every room."

This week was turning into her worst nightmare. Would it ever end?

"Why don't you text when it's safe for me to come

home," she suggested, filling him in on the ATV incident. At least she was in the clear with Hardy and, as it turned out, in the right for getting out of Dodge when she did.

"Will do," Hardy agreed, and they ended the call.

Glancing up at Brax was a mistake. The look in his eyes sent a different sensation skittering across her skin. No one had ever looked at her with eyes so determined to protect her, and she'd had a security detail since she'd made it in the business. There was another emotion in there that she couldn't quite pinpoint. Possessiveness? More of those butterflies released in her stomach and she didn't bother to fight the feeling this time.

The thought of Brax Firebrand being attracted to her was where she drew the line. She was reading too much into a look. He was one of the good ones and wouldn't take lightly to someone threatening her or anybody else for that matter. He'd shown up in the nick of time and had gotten her out of a tight spot. Of course she would feel a certain pull toward him for saving her.

It was as simple as that.

Besides, when did she become attracted to a Firebrand?

The feeling of being home must be more powerful than she realized. And she'd missed Lone Star Pass. Leaving all those years ago was like cutting off a piece of her heart. The thought of returning became harder and harder with her tour schedule. She was just beginning to realize the toll being away for so long was having on her.

"If I heard you correctly it's not safe for you to go back there," he said. A jaw muscle ticked, and it seemed like he was holding back something he really wanted to say.

"That's right. People got past Hardy," she admitted. "Everyone is accounted for and Hardy is clearing the house before I go home. Lucky me, he didn't realize I'd skipped out before it all went down. I'm in the clear."

Brax shook his head.

She shot him a confused look.

"What do you think about staying here at the ranch a while?" he asked.

"I don't want to leave the guys high and dry." What would that be saying to them? Her life was the only one worth saving?

Brax clenched his back teeth and the jaw muscle ticked again. He studied her for a long moment but must've decided not to speak his mind.

"Should we go inside now?" she asked. The honest truth was that she feared she would be putting his family in danger. It would only be a matter of time before her new location would be figured out, and an overzealous fan or reporter would find the holes in security at the ranch. As far as she knew poachers never came close to the houses or barns.

He took the couple of steps before opening the door. "After you."

"Should we call your mom and tell her I'm coming? I don't want to catch her off guard," she said.

"Are you kidding? And ruin the best surprise she's had all year?" He seemed to reconsider the comment when he mumbled, "Well, a close second."

She told herself not to ask about that later but figured it might have something to do with having a granddaughter.

"Funny, I don't think I've ever been in the main house before," she said as she walked past Brax and into an expansive kitchen. "Wow."

"Seems a shame the Marshall lived here alone for so

many years." He glanced around. "All this space going to waste."

"Can't say that I ever knew him very well," she admitted. "He was never rude to me if I ever ran into him in the barn or on the property. He never seemed to mind my presence. But I can't remember a time he ever really acknowledged me either."

"He was a complicated man. Or so I'm realizing more and more," Brax said.

"You said Adam lives here now." She didn't want to impose.

"Him and his family moved in," he said. "Hold on. I'll check and see where Mother is. Make yourself comfortable."

"Mind if I grab a glass of water?" she asked.

"Glasses are in the cabinet by the sink. Or bottled water is in the fridge." He motioned toward the farmhouse sink.

"I miss good old tap water," she said, thinking how amazing it would have been to have big family dinners in here and what a missed opportunity it had been for the Marshall. The man had been an enigma all right. He clearly loved his family in his own way and built multiple residences and two barns so they'd be at home here. But never had them in the main house. Not even Sunday supper, which was a big deal in these parts. "Always tasted better here on the ranch."

Raleigh was beginning to remember how great life had been at home. She'd blocked so much out and put blinders on for her career. Had she been in survival mode all this time? Was she really living?

"Hold tight." Brax couldn't wait to see the look on his mother's face when she saw who was standing in the kitchen. He heard voices down the hallway and found her with Prudence and Angel. All three sat on the floor in the once stiff formal living room that had been transported to a bright and colorful playroom.

There was a princess-themed teepee in one corner and the flooring was made of soft pieces that fit together like a puzzle. This place had been transformed in a matter of days thanks to internet shopping and next day shipping according to his mother. He couldn't remember the last time he'd see her with a smile this big on her face.

"How's it—" He stopped the minute his mother looked up at him. That same guilty look from earlier crossed her dark Italian features.

"Brax," she said quickly, like she was trying to cover the slip. She forced a smile that he figured was meant to look breezy. "What are you doing back so soon?"

"I have something you should see in the kitchen." He decided this wasn't the time to air out dirty laundry. But she would come clean with her secret soon.

"Oh?"

This wasn't the reaction he expected from his mother.

"Come on," he urged.

"I'll take Angel." Prudence smiled at the baby as his mother handed her over.

"You guys can come too," he said, figuring Prudence might be familiar with Raleigh, since they'd all attended the same schools. He figured the two had to be somewhere close in age.

Brax followed the trio down the hall.

"Hold on a minute," he said to his mother. He waved Prudence to go on but put an index finger to his lips so she wouldn't say a word when she saw the surprise. He turned his mother around to face him. "Hands over your eyes."

She stared at him for a long moment. If only he could see what was going on inside her head. She forced another smile and brought her hands up, but the look on her face was...fearful?

"Don't worry. This is a good surprise," he said to calm her rattled nerves.

With a hand on each shoulder, he turned her around and then walked her into the kitchen. "I'm going to let go of you but don't look until I tell you to, okay?"

She nodded and he could feel her trembling. This wasn't like her and now he was concerned. He decided to let the other subject drop for now but the two of them would have a conversation very soon.

He steadied her with his hands, shot a look toward Raleigh, and then said, "Open your eyes."

Mom gasped. She squealed and clapped her hands together, bringing them to her chest. "Raleigh? Is that really you?"

Raleigh practically beamed as she curtsied, and it was the first time she seemed truly happy since he ran into her last night. "It's so good to see you, Mrs. Firebrand."

"Oh my goodness." Mom threw her hands out and gaited toward the beautiful redhead. The two embraced and the sight warmed Brax's heart more than he wanted to admit.

Prudence stood next to the island with Angel cradled in her arms. She might not be the baby's biological parent, but she was Angel's mother in every sense of the word.

"How? When?" Mom didn't normally get so flustered she couldn't finish her sentence.

"Who wants a cup of coffee?" Prudence asked.

Mom whirled around. "I'll get it. Everyone sit down. This is a celebration." She turned back to Raleigh. "Can you stay for a little while?"

"Yes, ma'am," Raleigh said.

"No more of that formal nonsense," Mom said. "Call me Mom Firebrand just like you used to."

"Will do." Raleigh took a seat at the table near Prudence and it looked like a weight had lifted from her shoulders as well.

Brax helped his mother with the drinks.

"A good surprise?" he asked, noticing she had tears streaming down her cheeks.

"A very good one," she admitted. And then surprised him with, "A secret is killing me. I can't live like this." She turned to face him. "We need to talk later when it's just the two of us."

He nodded, wondering what that was all about.

To further his confusion, she stared straight into his eyes and whispered, "My beautiful boy."

With that, she sniffled twice and then started pouring coffee. He double-fisted a pair of mugs and his mom carried two more. She set one down in front of Raleigh as he tried to figure out what on earth his mom meant. If he'd been to the doctor lately, he'd be worried about bad test results after the way she looked at him.

"I can't believe you're here in the flesh," Mom said to Raleigh with a huge smile plastered on her face, and then her expression turned serious. "I'm so relieved you're okay."

"It's been a scary few days. That's for sure," Raleigh said on a sharp sigh. She picked up the mug and took a sip. "The coffee always was better here on the ranch. Why is that?"

"The well water," Mom quipped.

Brax noticed how deftly Raleigh had changed the

subject. Did she want to avoid talking about the bomb incident? Speaking of which, he needed to talk to her about filing a report with Sheriff Lawler about the ATV incident. The guy shouldn't be allowed to get away with chasing her like that. He might have been an obsessed fan or reporter. The likelihood he was the bomber had to be slim. How would he know where she was? Brax's hands fisted at thinking about what might have happened if he hadn't been right there or gone to check out the minibike sound and her cry for help.

"I've noticed it too," Prudence agreed. "And it's good to see you again, Raleigh."

"Likewise." Raleigh lifted her coffee mug and the ceramic clinked together.

"You two know each other?" Brax asked.

"We were in the same grade in school," Raleigh supplied.

"I didn't realize," he said.

"Because you were like four grades ahead of us." Raleigh laughed and the tension lines around her eyes relaxed. "You used to seem so much older to me back then."

He decided not to point out the fact that four years wasn't much of a gap at all while in their thirties.

"I remember seeing you with a notebook in your hand at all times," Prudence said to Raleigh. "I thought maybe you were going to be a writer someday. Turns out I was close."

Raleigh's cheeks flushed like they did when she was embarrassed. "You always had a book in your hand and I still can't believe we weren't friends."

"Leave it to two shy girls to spend years together in school without ever speaking," Prudence pointed out with a smile.

"True," Raleigh agreed.

"Tell me about your career," Mom said. "What's it like on the road?"

"The shows are great. The fans...amazing," she said. "Sleeping on a tour bus with seven messy guys isn't so much fun."

Mom laughed and nodded. She would know what it was like to have a mess of boys running around.

"Your daughter is beautiful." Raleigh motioned toward Angel. She changed the subject and he noted how little she liked to talk about herself. He figured someone with her fame would be all about themselves. She seemed like she'd rather talk about paint drying. Raleigh was turning out to be quite the contrast from what he anticipated. But then, what exactly had he expected? Definitely not the pull of attraction from someone who used to call him, 'Brat' instead of his name.

Speaking of mothers and their children, Mom's words were starting to haunt him. What kind of secret could have her this torn up inside? And why did she want to speak to him about it?

6

Raleigh needed to make and excuse and leave.

Being here at the main house with Mom Firebrand, Prudence and her baby, and Brax felt a little too good. Once the threat was over, she'd be back on the road, on the tour, and what? Heartsick for home?

No thanks. She needed to nip this situation in the bud before it had time to blossom. She looked at Mom Firebrand. So many happy memories flooded Raleigh. Before she left, she needed to say one thing.

"I wrote a tribute song for you," she said, fiddling with her coffee cup. For one, she felt bad about never circling back before and telling Mom Firebrand. Secondly, what if she didn't like it?

"Me?" So much warmth exuded from the older woman's eyes. They might be the window to the soul but they were also good at radiating someone's mood. "I'm honored."

"*If Only,*" Raleigh said. She hummed a few bars and then started in on the lyrics. She stopped after the first refrain. "Do you know that one?"

Mom Firebrand's eyes welled up. "Know it? It's one of my all-time favorites, even if I had no idea it was about me."

"Good damn song," Brax said low and under his breath.

"You listen to my music?" Raleigh didn't bother to hide her shock.

"Adam dragged me to a concert or two in Austin over the years." He took a sip of coffee, blocking his face. She couldn't read his expression and a piece of her really needed to see if he liked her music or not. It shouldn't mean so much to her, except this was home. Random people could hate her but the people she cared most about mattered. Their opinions mattered.

When he put the mug down, his expression was unreadable.

"It was good," he said, like he was sitting in front of a firing squad.

Of course, there were three sets of eyes staring at him expectantly.

"Pay no attention, sweetie," Mom said. "He loves your music."

He grinned and she wanted to reach over and give him a friendly tap on the arm like they'd done as kids when he'd been a pest.

She didn't figure reaching across his mother to slap his forearm would be appreciated, so she contained the urge. Her cell buzzed in her pocket, so she fished it out and checked the screen. "Excuse me."

Conversation was a low hum as she stood up and walked to the opposite side of the granite island anchoring the room.

"Hey, Hardy. What's up?" she immediately asked.

"The house is clear. I'm working with local authorities on getting a deputy parked out front while we're in town.

Should I come pick you up now?" Hardy's questions shouldn't cause a lead fireball to land in the pit of her stomach.

"No. Not yet," she said quickly. *Five more minutes.* "I'm still visiting. Okay if I text you with a plan?"

"Okay," he said but he sounded anything but.

Her security detail deserved an explanation.

"I need to have a conversation with Wade and I'd rather be away from the guys when I make the call. Nothing too big," she added. "Just personal stuff he's supposed to be handling for me that seems to be slipping through the cracks lately. Nothing to do with the band."

"We're here whenever you're ready to come back," Hardy said. "Or I can come stay with you wherever you are."

"No, thanks. That's not necessary here." The truth was that she wanted to step away from her life for a little while longer. Hardy was a reminder that she needed protection because someone was targeting her. The same icy chill from earlier raced down her spine thinking about it. "I gotta go. I'll text. I promise."

He barely got the word, *Okay*, out before she ended the call. The room suddenly felt stuffy and she needed air, recognizing the panic attack as it reared its ugly head. They were easier to conquer when she recognized them right away.

Back in the early days when she first started playing to crowds, she developed a bad case of stage fright. It had gotten bad enough for Sharon to bring a therapist on tour who'd taught Raleigh a few tricks.

This blip was nothing compared to the doozies she'd gone through. All this one took was a couple of slow breaths and a reminder she was fine. Everything was fine. She grounded herself by planting her palms on the cool granite either side of the farmhouse sink. She stared out the window onto the amazing land. The twin barns in the distance reminded her that everyone had two sides to them.

Before she could calm her racing heart, Brax stepped up behind her.

"Everything okay?" His voice traveled over her like fine silk. She could feel his strong male presence behind her without turning around. He was a foot behind her and she could hear his steady breathing.

"Give me a minute," she managed to say without her voice shaking. She didn't want him to know the effect he was having on her. "Hey, Brat."

Her attempt to bring levity to the moment failed miserably the minute her arms goosebumped. Electricity jolted through her when he touched her shoulder.

"Let me know if you need me," he said low and under his breath.

Boy, did that sentence cover so much more than he probably bargained for.

"Will do," was all she could manage to say through the haze that was Brax. A haze that had her wanting to turn around and press her lips to his. A haze that had her wishing she could reach out to him, lean into him. A haze that had her needing to feel his mouth moving against hers.

He stepped away and the room got cold. No one had had that kind of effect on her since...ever when she really thought about it.

No. No. No.

She couldn't afford to get attached to anyone or anything when she would just head out on the road again the minute this whole situation blew over. Between touring and making new music there was no time for anything or anyone else.

Crazy how the plan to work like mad to build her career

to a national level so she didn't have to be on the road most of the year hadn't worked out so well. If someone told her at thirty-two she'd still be grinding the tour or in the studio, she would have laughed at them. She was supposed to be able to slow down by this point.

Being on the road might be losing some of its shine but being with her fans never would. Her shows were everything. Or had they become everything?

It was probably the back-to-back concerts that were starting to wear thin because she couldn't allow herself to consider the fact her priorities might be changing. She'd wanted national stardom far too long to let go of the dream now. No one got to take that away from her, especially not some coward who'd rigged a bomb because he was too chicken to face her.

Where did all that come from?

She gripped the bullnose edge of the counter and took in a few deep breaths. This jerk didn't get to win.

With new resolve, she strode back to the table and reclaimed her seat. She looked at Prudence and then Mom Firebrand. "What did I miss?"

"Not much. We were just talking about inviting you to stay for lunch." Mom Firebrand broke out into a wide smile.

How could Raleigh let the woman who'd been a second mom to her down?

She glanced at Brax. "Are you sticking around?"

"A guy has to eat," he said with a smirk.

It was infuriating how much that look caused her heart to pound her ribcage from the inside out.

"Does that mean you're considering staying?" Mom Firebrand asked.

She knew better than to accept the invitation. It would be a mistake to get comfortable here. Leaving would be that much more difficult. She should cut bait now and save herself the heartache later.

"I'd hate to be the one to break up the band before a good meal," she said. "Please tell me you're making your famous meatballs."

So much for sticking to a plan.

BRAX NEEDED to bring in the sheriff. He'd meant to call before now. He also needed to talk to Raleigh about mentioning the incident to his family and ranch hands. Bronc Harris, ranch foremen, needed to be informed as well. The ATV jerk seemed willing to trespass on anyone's land and he could come back armed or with friends.

"Can I steal you for a sec?" he asked Raleigh.

"Yeah, sure." She glanced at Prudence and then his mother. "I'll be right back."

He led her into the former living room now playroom to get out of earshot.

"I've been thinking we should alert the sheriff to what happened earlier," he started.

She put up a hand to stop him from continuing.

"It's crazy enough as it is and everyone is on alert. What good would it do?" Her body stiffened and her words came out strained.

"We don't know how dangerous this guy is or if he plans to come back. I have to alert my family and I wouldn't be doing my job very well if I let our ranch hands or foreman walk into danger," he explained.

Raleigh issued a sharp sigh.

"You're right. That was pure selfishness on my part at not wanting to rile up my security detail more than I already have." Her shoulders deflated. "Of course, I want everyone here and in town to be safe."

"I'll send out a text," he said.

Her eyes widened and he could almost see the wheels churning. She shifted her weight from foot to foot.

"Actually, I know I said I'd stay for lunch, but I should probably head back home and tell Hardy we need to move on." It seemed to hit home that her presence might place everyone in danger.

"Don't do that," he said.

"What?" she asked.

"Retreat." His one word seemed to strike a chord.

"Hey, don't be a brat," she defended, fire in her emerald eyes.

"I'm not trying to upset you and I'm definitely not trying to run you off." His temper was rising and he had no idea why. He shouldn't care one way or the other if she stuck around. He shouldn't need to keep her safe more than he needed air. And he definitely shouldn't close the distance between them and kiss her.

"You guys would be better off without me here," she admitted and the flash of vulnerability in those green eyes hit him at the core.

He took a step toward her and locked gazes, searching for encouragement or rejection. When her tongue slicked across her bottom lip, leaving a silky trail in its wake, he decided encouragement. An urgency was building inside him that he knew better than to let run wild.

So, Brax closed the gap, bent down, and pressed his lips to hers. Electricity jolted as she brought her hands up to his shoulders. He half expected her to push him away. She dug her fingernails into his muscles instead. He interpreted the move as more encouragement.

A second later, he brought his hands up to cup her cheeks, tilting her head back for better access.

He kissed the freckle above her lip. Then, the one on her cheek before his lips found hers again. Suddenly, catching a breath was difficult as his chest squeezed and a dozen campfires lit inside him. She smelled like a mix of spring flowers after a morning rain and a field of peppermint. She tasted like dark roast. He liked coffee a whole lot better on her tongue.

Raleigh parted her lips more and he delved his tongue deeper in her mouth, tasting the sweet honey there.

His mind focused on one thing...*more*.

He wanted more of Raleigh. More of her taste. More of the way she touched him. More of the way she responded to him.

A clearing the throat noise from behind interrupted the moment.

"Hey, sorry, I was asked to get a special blanket and it's in here." Adam eased in, arm still in a sling. He seemed to make a special effort not to look directly at Brax or Raleigh.

"Great," Raleigh whispered.

"No problem, Adam. It's your home. Take what you need." Brax tried to play the moment off like it was nothing.

Adam grabbed a pink blanket with silk material wrapped around the edges. "Here it is. Got what I came for."

Awkward was a pretty good word to describe what was happening. Brax just wished he could shield Raleigh from the embarrassment of being caught during their first kiss. The first of many, he hoped.

"Yeah, no more kidding around, Brax," she said, taking a few steps toward the hallway, and tripping over her own two feet. She caught herself, hands on the wall, in time to avoid the embarrassment of face-planting. "We have to get back in there."

He was thrown for a loop with her comment.

"After you," he said, stuffing down the hit to his ego. "But, hey, Adam. Can you stick around for a second?"

"Yes, and Red Devil has been located and is tucked away in the equipment building for safe keeping, just like you asked," Adam reported.

"Thank you for seeing to it the minibike was taken care of," Brax said as Raleigh smiled her approval.

"I know the way." Raleigh pointed toward the kitchen. Her dramatic movements weren't helping draw less attention to the fact they'd been kissing a few seconds ago. And those had been some of the hottest, sexiest kisses he'd had in a long time. Maybe ever.

They'd been caught red-handed. Time to fess up.

"I'll be right in," he said to her before walking over and taking her hand in his. He lifted hers to his mouth and pressed a tender kiss there.

Locking gazes, he saw an emotion flicker behind her eyes that stirred an unfamiliar feeling in his chest.

And then she withdrew her hand like it had been burned, turned away from him, and couldn't get away from him fast enough.

7

"There might be troubling brewing on the ranch," Brax said to his brother.

"So, I saw," Adam responded with a wink and a smirk.

Brax waved the comment off.

"I'm being serious. And this might put people's lives in danger," Brax stated.

All playfulness left Adam's face. "What are we talking about here?"

"Raleigh is home because a bomb threat that turned out to be real shut down her tour for the time being. She thought she could slip into town unnoticed, but found out the hard way that wasn't going to happen," Brax explained.

"I'm guessing she's staying at the place she inherited from her grandmother," Adam said.

"That's right." Brax folded his arms and leaned against the doorjamb. "I found her at the barn last night."

"Up in the loft?" Adam's face brightened.

Brax nodded.

"I can't count the number of times I heard her up there

picking away at the guitar and writing in that notebook of hers." Adam smiled at the memory.

"I'm guessing she needed a quiet place. Somewhere to clear her mind after what happened," Brax presumed.

"And now she's concerned her presence might put us in the line of fire." Adam waved off the threat like it was no big deal.

Firebrands didn't scare easily.

"Caught a guy on an ATV trying to get to her earlier today," Brax admitted. "Might have been a fan. He didn't have a weapon and spooked with mine."

"The threat to her is real. I have no doubt about that," Adam said. "She's been getting national attention with this last album and there's a lot of anticipation around the next release."

Brax shook his head. "How do you know so much about her career?"

"Mom will tell anyone who will listen." Adam shrugged. "Plus, the woman practically grew up here at the ranch, even though she was quiet as a church mouse most of the time. Until she got on that minibike of hers. Plus, I like her music." Adam threw the baby blanket over his shoulder. "What's wrong with that? Our local girl has done well for herself. I'm proud as punch."

"She has talent," Brax agreed.

"And how many local folks put themselves out there like she did? She left town at eighteen…a baby." Adam made a tsk-tsk noise. "I overheard her grandmother and Mom chewing on that for a long time."

"Not to change the subject but speaking of our mother, she said she wants to speak to me in private. Says something heavy has been weighing on her mind. Any idea what she might be talking about?" Brax didn't think his brother would have an answer but it was worth a shot.

Adam put his hands up in the surrender position. Moving his right arm caused him to wince in pain.

"How much longer do you have to wear that sling?" he asked.

"Another day is too long if you ask me. Knife cuts hurt the most. Ever notice that?" Adam asked.

Brax laughed.

"We probably shouldn't have played with them when we were kids," he said.

Adam shook his head.

"The first mistake our parents made was telling us not to." Adam regained his casual smile.

"It's a good thing you have a daughter," Brax stated. "We already have enough testosterone in this place."

"Speaking of which, have you heard from Kellan?" Adam asked.

"Not much since I overheard him talking about the divorce papers needing signed. At least, that's the last I heard. He never told me about it personally," Brax admitted.

"He thinks he's too good to talk to anyone on this side of the family now that his side inherited mineral rights after the Marshall's death," Adam said.

"Too bad they can't drill without our permission." Brax couldn't help but smile a little bit at the situation despite the heavier mood.

The Marshall had put his fighting sons in a precarious position. He bequeathed the ranch and cattle to Brax's father and the mineral rights to Kellan's dad. The law stated the owner had to give express permission to drill on their land, so Kellan's side of the family couldn't do anything with their precious mineral rights without permission from Brax's dad. The brothers were fire and gasoline, so coming to a compromise didn't seem likely in this lifetime. Proof the Marshall had a sense of humor behind a tough as nails exterior.

Of course, the Marshall had done nothing but encourage his sons to compete against each other since the days they were born. So, he was probably looking on with a smirk on his face.

The other kink in the plan stated if the last grandson married before an agreement could be reached then all the land, cattle, and rights was to be split equally among Brax's generation.

Most of the Firebrand men were committed to single life in the near future. A couple had already gone through, or were in the process of, a divorce. So, that was about as likely to happen as a snowstorm in August. But it did light a different kind of fire under the elder Firebrand men's backsides. It told them they didn't have forever to dicker around.

Adam reached up with his good arm and scratched his head.

"As far as Raleigh is concerned, she's like one of the family and we always take care of family," Adam said.

"My thoughts exactly," Brax said. "Except she doesn't see it that way. From her perspective, she sees it as putting people she cares about in harm's way."

"Well, I guess I can't blame her when you put it like that," Adam stated. "We'll think of something to say to help her see the light."

With her stubborn streak, that was easier said than done. He also took note of what Adam had said about the pressure on her new album. She handled it all well. The lifestyle. The fame.

He needed to pick her brain a little bit to see if he could

help figure out who in her circle might not want her to succeed. An overzealous fan upset she wasn't releasing music fast enough? Or not happy with her songs or the direction of her career?

His mind snapped to Selena Quintanilla, a promising young Latina singer, also from Texas, who was murdered by the person who started her first fan club. He made a mental note to ask about any fan clubs Raleigh knew about or interacted with.

"You better take the blanket to Angel." Brax nodded toward Adam's shoulder.

"When are you planning to send out the text?" Adam asked.

"Now, before I head back to the kitchen. People need to know as soon as possible," Brax said.

"I'll save you a place at the table for lunch." Adam patted Brax on the shoulder as he started toward the hallways. He paused and seemed to be searching for the right words. He seemed to settle on, "Just be careful, man. Okay?"

"Always."

Brax fished his cell from his pocket. He pulled up the ranch group message so he could include everyone in one shot. He entered the description of the ATV driver as best as he could. From the distance and with the trees, Brax had a general idea of what the guy had looked like. The most important thing was to get an alert out. Then, everyone would be on the lookout for a suspicious person.

His second text mentioned there was a VIP on the property who was a target.

Guesses filled up the chat in two seconds. All but one hit a bullseye. Casey's guess was out in left field. But then, the ranch hand wasn't getting a whole lot of sleep when he went home on weekends considering he had a newborn. After being around Angel, who held Brax's heart with her pinky finger, Brax realized how much work those little buggers were. He'd heard the term, *sleep like a baby*, and would never look at it the same again. Apparently, that meant sleep in three hours bursts twenty-four hours a day. No days off. No change in schedule. Just sleep, feed, and repeat.

He issued a sharp sigh. Great for Adam, not so much for Brax.

By the time he jotted a few notes into an app on his phone before he forgot, the hum of chatter floated down the hallway from the kitchen. So did the smell of Mom's meatballs. Hunger and curiosity got his boots headed down the hallway.

A half dozen Firebrands added to the five who were already there. Chatter was loud and his heart skipped a few beats when he didn't see Raleigh sitting there. For a split second, he feared she might havc gonc on home.

He walked through the crowd toward the table where he'd last seen her. She wasn't there either.

And then he caught sight of her by the sink on the other side of the island. His brother, Corbin, entered through the back door with his guitar.

Raleigh caught Brax's gaze from across the room and shot him the most helpless look before recovering with the smile that had looked genuine to him when he'd seen it on stage. Now, he wasn't so sure it wasn't the performer in her acting.

Brax cut through the crowd and then took her by the hand.

"Excuse us," he said to several not-so-thrilled faces as he walked her out the back door.

"Before we say anything or things get awkward between us, what happened in the playroom was a mistake," Raleigh started right in. She didn't want to blow a good thing and having Brax on her side definitely qualified.

"Agreed," he said.

She blinked a couple of times unsure she'd heard him right.

"I said we made a mistake," she clarified.

"Yes," he stated.

Those kisses were embedded in her thoughts, his lips branded hers. And how was she supposed to follow up that kind of chemistry?

"It's just, it's good being home and I got carried away in the moment remembering how amazing it was here and missing this place," she continued, talking so fast she tripped over a couple of her words.

"Won't happen again," he said.

Shouldn't he be a little put off by her rejection? She wasn't trying to be indignant but she was a pretty decent kisser. Or at least, others told her so. Had they been lying? Was she mediocre?

Now, her cheeks really burned.

"I'm sorry if I wasn't up to your usual standards," she said with a little more ire than she'd planned. Yes, she was poking the bear.

The bear chuckled.

"What's so funny?" she asked.

"I can't figure out if you're trying to let me down easy or put yourself down." He shrugged and those infuriatingly blue eyes of his held her gaze. The air crackled between them as if it wasn't hot enough in the middle of June at lunchtime.

"Let you down easy," she decided and all the fight left

her. "Those kisses were pretty great. I'm not going to lie. But they can't happen again."

"I'm clear on the point, Raleigh." And why did her name have to sound so good rolling off his tongue?

"I didn't realize how homesick I was until now and I don't want to confuse an attraction for missing this place." She waved her arms in the air. "Does that make sense?"

"Sure does," he said with a cocky grin.

"What's that look about?" She balled her fists and planted them on her hips.

"Nothing," he countered.

"It must mean *something*." She couldn't seem to let it go now that she'd gone down the path.

He shrugged.

She was ready to scream. A few deep breaths later and her pulse calmed down a few notches.

Raleigh started pacing the length of the house and back. She needed to burn off some of her pent-up energy.

"You've had a rough couple of days," Brax started with that whiskey in front of a roaring fire voice. "I'd planned on inviting you to stay at the main house with me but if the 'me' part makes you uncomfortable I can grab one of my brothers or cousins."

She stopped for a long moment, wishing it was that simple. "I just can't, Brax."

"Is it me?" he asked and it was the first hint of vulnerability in his voice.

"No. Yes. Kind of. It's you and your beautiful family," she said. "I would never forgive myself if something happened to any one of you because of me."

"Adam and I talked it over and we're comfortable with the risk," he said. "The rest of the guys would feel the same way because we view you as one of us."

Having someone around who had her back for a change threatened to disarm her defenses. She didn't get where she was in her career by sticking around one place too long or letting anyone in. Based on those smokin' hot kisses and the attraction sizzling between her and Brax, she could get into real trouble if she stayed at the ranch.

"Your band is welcome and whoever else is traveling with you," he continued. "It'd be a shame for all this room to go to waste."

Well, now she really needed to give it some thought. She chewed on her thumbnail.

Brax took her hand in his. "Think about it. You can go somewhere else, but your fans will find you. They've already proven how quickly that can happen."

He was saying all the right things to make her pause and think about it.

"I'm afraid we'd be in the way," she hedged but it was a lame excuse. This place was massive.

"You and the guys could take over the west wing of the main house. I'll grab a room next door to yours, so we'd have a wall in between us," he continued. The spark in his eyes said he knew he was making progress with her. Why did he have to have such pure blue eyes? And be so damn tempting?

"I mean, it's possible. It could work. I have a few songs due or we'll have to push back my next album's release. That'll upset a whole lot of people, and I hate the idea of letting down my fans." Could she stay at the Firebrand Ranch? The guys in the band would love it here. No question. They'd each have their own room—which she knew they'd see as a definite plus—and there was enough security that Hardy would have backup.

"I'd have to talk it over with the guys...my security guy

would have to give final approval." She didn't want to make Hardy's job any harder than it already was.

"Does that mean you'll seriously consider it?" Again, that spark in his eyes made turning down his offer next to impossible.

But it didn't change the fact that she wasn't sure that she could sleep in the room next to his without wanting to knock on his door...

8

"I'll talk it over with the guys," Raleigh promised and Brax's heart stirred. Being the one to ease her fears felt a little too right.

"Invite 'em over now for Mom's meatballs," he said. "That would seal the deal."

She laughed and his chest swelled with pride at being the one to break some of the tension for her in what had to be one helluva week.

"I'll call and see what they say." She let go of his hand and fished her cell phone out of her back pocket.

As she walked away, he had to force his gaze off her sweet, round bottom.

Great job keeping it in check, buddy.

What could he say? Raleigh had grown into a beautiful woman. She had always been sharp and smart women were sexy as hell. Her feistiness only added to her appeal. What was it about redheads?

Brax had a soft spot for a sexy, smart, feisty woman. Too bad Raleigh fit the bill to a T. He had no plans to settle down anytime soon but could see himself with someone like her at some point way down the road.

Of course, Raleigh would be long gone by then. Heck, she'd be out of Dodge in a week give or take, so there was no threat this attraction would go any further. It sure felt good for now. Inconvenient as all get out that he found himself drawn to someone he knew better than to try to date.

Besides, she was most likely propositioned every night of the week while on tour, which was practically all the time. He wasn't certain his ego could take the hits.

She spun around with a smile on her face that would melt ice in the freezer. She nodded and he took it to mean she got approval. A few seconds later, she ended the call and tucked her phone in her back pocket. A pair of jeans and boots had never looked so good on a person. Legs that went on for days. Legs he could envision tangled in bedsheets on a lazy Sunday morning.

Brax gave himself a mental shake.

"I take it your security detail approves," he said.

"Yes." She walked right up to him and placed her hands on his chest. With a big smile, she said, "I love being at Nana's but waking up to the scene right outside my window this morning wasn't good. Being here is the next best thing and the first time I've felt truly safe in a very long time. So, thank you."

Those words were the equivalent of standing next to a roaring campfire on a cold day.

"If you want me to stop kissing you, it would be a good idea to keep your lips as far away from mine as possible," he teased.

"Who said I *wanted* to stop? I believe I said it can't happen again. Two totally different things," she quipped with a wink before heading toward the backdoor.

He stood there, mute. A whole bunch of unholy thoughts roared through his brain.

She stopped at the door and turned around.

"Are you coming with me, or are you set on standing out here all day?" she asked.

Brax bit down on his bottom lip to stop from saying the first thing that popped into his mind about what he'd *like* to do that involved her.

"On my way."

The woman seemed to know exactly what to say to torture Brax in the best possible way. This seemed like a good time to remind himself they weren't dating, and nor would they be. They were nothing more than ships passing. He was providing a safe haven in a storm and she would be back on the road in no time.

He opened the door for her and she rewarded him with another one of those incredible smiles that was a sucker punch, square in the chest. She took his breath away.

Brax followed Raleigh inside to the small family gathering that had developed as soon as word got out she was home. She walked over to Corbin.

"Mind if I borrow that?" She pointed toward his guitar.

He handed over the acoustical piece with a ready smile. "Be my guest."

Brax leaned against the counter, preferring to stick to the back of the room near the door. He fired off a few texts to clear the way for her band with front gate security. His next text was to Steven Paine, head of security. Brax requested reinforcements after explaining there was a high profile individual staying at the main house with a few of her friends.

Paine's response was immediate.

On it.

As Brax looked up, he saw Raleigh sitting on the solid wood table with her boots on the seat of a chair. She started strumming the guitar and then broke into one of his favorite songs. Her voice trailed over him and through him, leaving nothing untouched. She might be worried about a fan breaching the gates of Firebrand Ranch, but the only real danger for Brax was the woman who sat in front of him, strumming the guitar.

The song ended and the room erupted. Her cheeks turned six shades of red before she went into another one of her biggest hits.

Adam strolled over, cradling Angel in his good arm. He had that Cheshire cat grin.

"Before you get too excited, nothing really happened," Brax said to his brother.

"Not what I saw." Adam stopped next to Brax and leaned against the same counter. They both faced Raleigh.

It didn't help matters that she glanced up, caught Brax's gaze, and smiled one of those knowing smiles that made it seem like the two of them were in on a secret.

"Shelter in a storm," Brax said under his breath, but loud enough for his brother to hear.

"That was some shelter," Adam teased.

"You should have seen the storm," was all Brax said before smiling back at Raleigh.

She cocked a brow, her movements so subtle he doubted anyone else realized what was going on between the two of them. Well, everyone except for Adam who picked that moment to elbow Brax in the ribs.

Corbin walked over about the same time. Now, his eyebrow raised.

"What's going on over here?" he asked.

"You see," Adam started, "there was this big storm." He stopped and elbowed Brax again. "He'll tell you all about it."

"Not me," Brax pushed off the counter, pocketed a shiny red apple from the basket on the counter, and slipped out back. He needed to check on Bullet anyway.

Besides, he needed to clear his head so he could think. Getting Raleigh alone to talk, especially once her band arrived, might prove more difficult than he wanted it to be. He also just remembered he hadn't called Sheriff Lawler yet.

He made the call as he headed to the barn. Lawler didn't pick up so Brax left a message stating what had happened and describing the ATV driver to the best of his ability. The truth be told, Brax didn't get a good look at the guy's face. He was on the thin side, though, and he wore a hoodie despite the ninety-degree temps. Other than that, he had on jeans. Maybe the sheriff could get some DNA from the trees and get a positive ID.

It was possible this guy could be the bomber, coming at Raleigh with a more direct approach this time. Every muscle in Brax's body tensed at the thought of someone trying to harm her. Again, what could a random person have to gain from killing her?

A sick kind of fame, he guessed. Whoever got to her would make headlines. The click-bait practically wrote itself.

Bullet needed exercise. He didn't bother to bridle her. She would follow him anywhere, especially when he had an apple in his pocket. He fished it out and shined it on his shirt after opening the gate to her stall. She whinnied and rocked her head up and down. She stamped her right hoof and then took a couple of steps toward him.

He held the apple in the air on his flat palm.

"This what you want?" he asked, taking a couple of steps backward.

Bullet nickered.

"Come and get it." He stepped back again and she followed. He walked her to the corral, easily accessible by the back door of the barn. Outside, the sun caused him to squint as he held out the apple for her nibble on.

Bite by bite, she polished off her favorite treat.

"Now, go on," he patted her back side and she took off in a trot. She circled the corral a few times, head high.

Brax walked over to the fence, climbed up, and perched. He sat there, watching his horse stretch her legs.

Out of the corner of his eyes, he saw the glint of metal. Instinctively, he reached for his pistol before realizing he wasn't wearing his holster. No one would leave a gun lying around in the barn. Gun safety was important on the ranch.

He bit out a curse as he hopped down, figuring he didn't need to give this jerk a clean shot. He whistled for Bullet to return. There were times she was too spunky to listen. The apple bribe had put her in a good mood. She trotted over.

Brax grabbed onto the base of her mane and jumped on, bareback. "Let's go."

RALEIGH SEARCHED the room for Brax. Concern tightened her chest when she couldn't find him.

Normally, she would keep on playing. This was home. She didn't have to play through. So, she finished the song and handed Corbin his guitar.

"Has anyone seen Brax?" She climbed off the table.

"I saw him leave twenty minutes ago," Mom Firebrand said. "Does anyone know if he came back?"

Heads shook in unison.

"Meatballs are ready. How about everyone sit down for lunch?" Mom Firebrand motioned toward the table with a bowl filled to the brim.

"If these taste half as good as they smell..." Raleigh's gaze flew to Adam as he checked his phone.

He glanced up at her and gave a small headshake before firing off a text.

The doorbell rang. She smiled at Mom Firebrand.

"My guys never miss a good meal," she said, following Corbin down the hallway.

Raleigh strode up beside him. "I didn't see Fallon. Is he here?"

"He signed up for the military and then went into Spec Ops." Corbin shook his head. "Said he didn't want to stick around here with all the fighting."

She shot him a questioning look after nodding.

"Special Forces operations," he clarified.

"As in a Navy SEAL?" Fallon had always been one of the popular guys, much like the other Firebrands. Corbin was different, when she really thought about it. He always seemed more serious about school. At least, from a distance.

"Yes. On the rare times he graces us with his presence, he doesn't talk about it though," Corbin said.

"That's pretty cool actually." She wondered what he must go through that kept the subject off limits. To be fair, he might just want a break. To really be home when he visited and leave work behind. She couldn't fault him for that.

"I had no idea things were that bad with your family," she admitted. To be fair, she was a visitor and spent most of her time with their mother.

"Yeah, it's a shame. Our father and uncle disagree more

often than not, and the Marshall seemed content to stoke the flame." He paused at the front door before opening and inviting her band in. "A lot is about to change and I doubt in a good way."

Corbin welcomed the guys inside.

"What is that smell?" Randy would be the first to notice.

"Homemade meatballs," she said. "Follow me to the food."

She purposely led to avoid being stuck in the back with Hardy. She'd met his eyes once already and there was a big conversation coming based on the intensity in his. Yes, they needed to sit down and have a one-on-one. Right now, she wanted everyone to be safe and to figure out where Brax had gone.

Slipping outside while everyone was distracted and eating wouldn't cut it. She'd learned her lesson after the ATV incident earlier.

The minute she set foot in the kitchen, she searched for Adam. Now, he was gone too.

Panic squeezed her chest but she forced a smile. She thought about sending Brax or Adam a text, and realized she had neither number. Asking Mom Firebrand for it seemed out of place.

She took in a slow, deep breath and then had everyone introduce themselves. Kenny took the seat next to hers.

"How'd you get out of the house so fast this morning?" he whispered.

"Got up early," she said.

"That's strange. You've never been an early riser," he pointed out. Being on tour together meant everyone knew each other's habits.

"Nope. Things are changing," she said as she accepted the big bowl being passed around. She plunked a couple of meatballs on her plate and then kept the bowl moving. Next, came spaghetti noodles and sauce. She turned to Mom Firebrand, who sat on Raleigh's left, and said, "You must keep a batch of these made up at all times. There's no way you just fixed these."

Mom Firebrand winked and threw her hands in the air.

"With this many mouths to feed, you learn a few tricks," she said. Raleigh had seen Mom Firebrand work her magic in the kitchen. Whenever she made sauce, she made tons in a huge pot, spending hours cooking it before leaving it overnight to settle. Then, she added grappa before portioning up and freezing, so that she always had some available in case of emergencies.

Raleigh could believe it. She'd never really seen herself as having a large family. In fact, had she ever really seen herself with a family at all?

It sounded crazy, even to her, but she hadn't given it much thought. Being too busy was a copout. It was true but everyone had five minutes here and there to contemplate life. She usually took a nap or wrote a song. The desire for kids had never really struck until the moment she saw Angel. Having Brax in the same room with a newborn caused a maternal reaction internally that she hadn't known she was capable of.

Could ovaries actually ache?

Because suddenly, she was envisioning him holding their newborn and that was exactly the moment she realized she'd lost her mind. The pressure of constantly being on the road or in the studio, plus now with the bomb threat, must mean she was hitting a hard wall. Having a husband or a family hadn't occurred to her. Besides, she had the band and the road crew. They were like family.

At times, she already felt like a mother with seven boys.

In that way, she could relate to Mom Firebrand. In fact, while Raleigh was here, she might as well get some tips from an expert.

"Is there something wrong with the food, honey?" Mom Firebrand's forehead creased with concern.

"No. It's even better than I remembered." The comment shocked her out of her deep thoughts.

"Then why are you pushing the meatball around with your fork instead of eating it?" Mom Firebrand could be counted on for stating facts. It was one of many things Raleigh loved about the older woman.

"Oh. I didn't realize I was," she said by way of defense. She lowered her voice when she added, "I'm just a little worried about Brax. It's not like him to miss a meal."

9

Brax hopped off Bullet. His cell was going crazy, buzzing in his pocket every two seconds and he needed to find out what was on fire. His mind snapped to the ATV driver or the bomber getting to Raleigh. Fire licked through his veins.

The screen said there were four missed calls from Adam and multiple text messages. Brax skimmed the texts. Realization dawned that he hadn't told anyone where he was going. He wasn't used to telling anyone his whereabouts but that needed to change.

There was a serious threat on the loose. Brax bit back a curse at worrying his brother. Besides, whoever was in the trees must've fled. That, or he was seeing things.

He called Adam.

"Hey, sorry. I'm good. Thought I saw something in the tree line so I came out to investigate. Now I'm not so sure anyone was out here in the first place," he explained.

"Good to know. I can back you up next time." Adam's offer was a polite way of saying Brax shouldn't be chasing anyone without backup.

"You're right. I should've clued you in. My bad. Won't happen again." Brax wouldn't run off chasing any more ghosts without a heads-up. It was the reason they had a group text.

"Cool." Adam lowered his voice and said, "Someone else hasn't stopped looking for you."

"Really?" He was caught off guard.

"That's right," Adam said. "You might want to make an appearance so she can stop watching the backdoor."

"On my way." Brax ended the call.

Bullet had had enough exercise. She'd be ready to munch on hay and hydrate. Brax took it easy on the ride back to give her a chance to cool down. It had been a while since he'd ridden bareback and he was reminded how much he preferred it. There was something pure about riding without a saddle or tack.

He led her back into the barn and then hopped down.

"We still got it, old girl." He patted his Paint horse on the neck.

She whinnied in response. There were times, like this one, where Brax would swear she could understand everything he said.

After taking care of his first love, he walked to the main house. Raleigh's concern was nothing more than her conscious feeling like she'd put his family in harm's way. She'd been concerned about bringing the bomber to the ranch.

So, he probably should've let her in on the fact he was stepping out. For the time being, he needed to get used to keeping everyone up to date on his activities and vice versa. The thought made him want to loosen his collar.

Brax loved the land and, almost more than that, his freedom.

This was a temporary situation, he reminded himself. What he didn't like was the temporary nature of spending time with Raleigh. Hers was a life of constant travel, concert dates booked a year in advance, and squeezing in time to record.

It sounded like a prison to him. But then, he was used to wide-open skies and the ability to come and go as he saw fit.

Despite knowing there could never be anything more between them, his traitorous heart still beat double-time the minute he stepped inside the kitchen and her gaze found his. What did the heart know? Wasn't that what half of the country songs were about anyway? Missed love. Missing love. Being hurt by love.

Brax was picking up on a common theme.

Raleigh stood up and walked over to him, all eyes followed her.

"Hey, everything okay?" she asked, leaning her hip against the counter. She stood so close he could breathe in her flowery scent, which wasn't such a good thing for a man who was trying to keep his distance.

From behind her, he caught someone he didn't recognize watching their interaction like it was a prize fight and one of the boxers was on the brink. Brax took note of the guy, especially the hard lines of his face as he studied Brax like he was sizing him up.

"I went to the barn to exercise Bullet." He expected the admission to make his collar feel a little too tight. Surprisingly, it didn't. But then, he'd put the situation in perspective before walking in the house.

"Oh." She didn't meet his gaze. "I was worried when I didn't see you. It's probably just the situation taking a toll, making me feel the need to know where everyone is at all times. I overreacted."

"Who could blame you; I would have done the same if you'd up and disappeared without a word," he said.

"Really?" She glanced up at him and those emerald eyes sparked.

"Of course," he reassured.

"Next time you head out to the barn, will you take me?" The tile floor suddenly got very interesting.

"I can do that," he said.

"I'd appreciate it. I write so much better in the loft and," she glanced around the room, "away from all the 'excitement.'"

He followed her trail. It seemed everyone had some interest in where she stood. Another job hazard, he figured. The not-so-glamorous side of fame.

"How about heading over now?" He wished he could rein the question in. Impulse had him wanting to help her escape even if only for a little while.

"I'd like that a lot actually. You don't mind? I thought you just came from there," she said.

"I'd take being in a barn any day to this." He held up his arms.

"This will probably sound crazy coming from me, but I know what you mean." She rewarded him with the kind of smile that melted too many of his defenses in one fell swoop.

He reached out for her hand, and then linked their fingers.

The hotshot who'd been giving them the eye the whole time tossed his napkin onto the table. Brax made a mental note to ask what her relationship was with each of her band members.

"I better let Hardy know our plans," she said with an infectious smile.

"I'll wait right here."

She nodded before practically trotting over to her security detail.

Hardy was youngish and had a decent size to him. His weapon was visible from his shoulder holster. Brax's mother generally had a no-guns-inside-the-house policy but she seemed to be willing to make an exception for Raleigh. This seemed to come with the territory of hosting someone famous.

Brax studied each of the new faces that he could see from the vantage point behind the island as he made a meatball sandwich. Adam came over and joined him as he took the first bite.

"Sorry about having to track you down," Adam started.

Brax shook his head. "Don't be. We have to get used to staying in touch while there's a threat."

"Raleigh sure looks relieved you came back," Adam pointed out.

"Doesn't mean anything except friendship," Brax said.

"All right. You want to play it that way, it's cool." Adam's smirk wasn't helping matters.

"Aren't you busy with your new wife and new daughter?" Brax said.

"Never too busy to give you a hard time, brother." Adam threw a shoulder into Brax and then winced in pain.

"I don't feel a bit sorry for you," Brax teased. "You had that coming."

"That's fair." Adam turned to face the window above the sink, standing side-by-side with Brax. "Kenny might be a problem."

"Hotshot over there?" Brax said low and under his breath.

"He's the drummer in the band. From what I can gather, he has a thing for Raleigh like nobody's business."

"I noticed the same thing two seconds after I walked into the kitchen," Brax admitted.

"He got real sour when he saw her talking to you," Adam said.

"Then, my next move is really going cause him heartache." Brax took another bite of meatball sandwich, chewed on it.

"What's that, lover boy?" Adam teased.

"First of all…no." That was all Brax had to say. "Second of all, she wants to head up to the loft and doesn't want to freak anybody out by going by herself."

"Try not to come back with so much lipstick next time. Okay?" Adam ribbed Brax with the same shoulder move. "Had that one coming too. It was worth it, by the way."

Adam walked toward Prudence, who was giving their daughter a bottle.

Brax polished off the meatball sandwich as the big guy stood up.

Raleigh returned, rolling her eyes.

"Looks like we have company." She hitched her thumb behind her as the guy thanked Brax's mom for the food and then followed Raleigh.

"Ready?" he asked after introducing himself and shaking hands.

"Hold on." Raleigh held up a finger. She walked over to Corbin and motioned toward his guitar.

He smiled before handing it over.

Kenny glared at Brax, which almost caused him to laugh. He didn't want to brag, but he was a whole lot bigger and meaner than the drummer. It wouldn't exactly be fair if the guy tried to pick a fight.

The guy also registered as someone to watch and maybe warn Raleigh about. It warranted a discussion at the very least. Just to push the guy's buttons, Brax took the guitar from Raleigh and then threw his free arm around her shoulders as they exited.

Yes, Brax was being dramatic with the move but Hotshot was on his radar and he wanted to get a reaction from the guy. To gauge how far he would go if pushed.

"Mind if Hardy clears the barn?" Raleigh could feel her cheeks warm.

"Go for it." Brax opened the door. "Watch the stables. Some of the horses spook easily."

Hardy thanked him and walked inside.

"Sorry about this." Raleigh motioned toward Hardy as he walked inside.

"Don't worry about it." Brax's expression said the opposite, but she didn't think this was the time to call him out.

"I really appreciate it. I've put him through a lot in the past twenty-four hours and I'm trying to make it up to him by giving him a little more of the reins."

"I'm not a big fan of someone I don't know carrying a weapon on our property," Brax admitted. "But if it keeps you here, I'm willing to make an exception."

She'd been clear where she stood on a relationship, so she needed to be strong on her convictions. Except the pull to Brax was stronger than anything she'd ever felt. Even his scent drew her in, all spicy and male. His warmth made her want to take a step closer, like she was walking into the sun.

She loved the sun.

After a few minutes, Hardy appeared in the opened doorway.

"All good," he said.

"Thanks. Why don't you stand out here and make sure it stays that way?" Raleigh had no intention of allowing Hardy inside the barn while she tried to write.

"Yes, ma'am." Hardy seemed pleased with the compromise, and he was there to do a job after all.

Raleigh scooted inside and went straight to the loft. She climbed the spiral staircase and her mood lightened. It was like she had on fifteen winter coats and one came off with each step.

"I love this place," she said.

The arched ceiling made it possible for Brax to stand up. There were a couple of hay bales pushed up against one wall. Someone had brought a couple of cartons up here at one point and they made for comfortable seating. But her favorite spot was smack in the middle, sitting on the floor with her legs crisscrossed, hunkered over a guitar.

She planted herself down and then propped her arms up on the guitar.

"So, tell me something about you," she said to Brax.

"Like what?" His eyebrow arched.

"You tell me," she said. "Anything."

"I hated school," he said.

"Same here. Mrs. Wriggles was the meanest teacher I've ever seen," she said on a sigh.

"Sure made seventh grade harder than it had to be," he agreed.

"Is she still around?" she asked.

"I think she retired a couple of years ago. Seems like I overheard Mom talking about it," he said.

"Lone Star Pass education system is the better for it."

She laughed for the first time in a really long time. It was the kind that bubbled up from her stomach and tickled her throat on the way up.

"You can say that again," he said. "I had a lot of good teachers, to be fair. School just wasn't for me."

"As I remember, you were pretty good at it," she said, realizing she might have just given away the fact she'd kept tabs on him back then.

"I'm good at a lot of things I don't care for," he said. "Sometimes in life, you just have to put your head down and get through something unpleasant."

"Well, that's a true statement if ever I've heard one," she agreed. "The minute I graduated, I hit the road."

"Why is that?" He cocked his head to one side. The move sent a half dozen butterflies flitting around in her stomach.

"I needed to go. Start my career. I'd had this thing burning in my chest for so many years and Nana kept reeling me back in. She told me I could do anything I wanted the day I turned eighteen and graduated." She smiled at the memory. On the road, she always pushed thoughts of Nana aside for fear they'd crush her. Talking about her here with Brax felt right.

"Didn't you turn eighteen on graduation day?" he asked.

"Yep." She wiggled her eyebrows and was rewarded with a genuine smile. "My bags were already packed. Not that I was eager or anything."

"You made her proud," he said and his comment filled her with warmth.

"I really hope so. She was everything to me. Grandmother. Mother. Father. Best friend. I can't imagine how my life would have turned out without her." A surprising tear sprang to her eye. Not a tear of sadness but of remembering. There'd been so many good times in this town.

"You were all she ever talked about." He smiled in a show of perfectly white, perfectly straight teeth.

"My music and Nana are all I had." She didn't mean for that to come out like she was feeling sorry for herself. "Don't get me wrong, I love both more than life itself."

"No relationships?" His expression turned serious despite the fact he broke eye contact.

"Nothing worth reporting back." Admitting her lack of a love life to Brax heated her cheeks.

"Mind if I ask about your relationship with your drummer?" This time, he looked up and she realized he'd picked up on something.

10

Brax shouldn't be hanging on the edge of his seat for Raleigh's answer. And yet there he was, doing just that.

"We're in a band together," she stated, picking up a piece of hay and picking at it with her fingers. "We've spent a lot of time together."

"Is that all?"

"We dated a hundred years ago but that's been over for a long time." She rattled off the words quickly, like she didn't want to get talking about it over with as fast as possible.

"Does he know that?" The question had to be asked. The fact she didn't answer right away told him everything he needed to know.

"I've been clear with him there's no chance of getting back together." She blew out a frustrated-sounding breath.

"He's not getting the message, is he?" Brax could feel his muscles tense up, and yet he didn't have any designs on Raleigh. She was free to date anyone she wanted.

Which was the problem, an annoying little voice in the

back of his mind pointed out. She didn't want to date Hotshot.

"He will," she said with the kind of confidence that showed her conviction.

"How long have you known him?" Brax needed to see how far their relationship went back for the investigation. Or so, he told himself this wasn't personal.

"Since the beginning. And that's when we dated," she said. "It didn't work out between us. We moved on. He got married..."

"When was the divorce final?" he asked, figuring that had to be the case.

"Recently. And that's when he made it clear that he wanted to start things up again," she said. "It just doesn't work like that for me. I told him the truth and he's been trying to win me over ever since."

"How hard is he trying?" Based on the glares from earlier, the guy wasn't letting go.

"It gets uncomfortable at times but I put my foot down. Believe it or not, I've gotten really good at taking care of myself." Those last words came out sounding defensive. She crossed her arms over the guitar, a sign she was closing up.

"I have no doubt you can take of yourself and probably everyone else around you." He meant every word. "I just don't think you should always have to."

She blew out a breath.

"I love these guys. So, don't get me wrong. But sometimes I feel like their mother and I don't even want kids." Her comment surprised him.

He decided not to comment. When he really thought about it, her lifestyle of being on the road or in the studio wouldn't give her a whole lot of time for anything else.

"We live in small quarters, on the same bus, together almost three hundred and sixty-five days a year," she said.

"You don't take any time off from touring?"

"Kind of, but I'm making music so it's not really time off so to speak," she said. He must've shot some look at her because she added, "Do you take vacations from the ranch?"

"I'll take that as a no," he said, smiling. "But I'll add that when you love what you do it's not called work."

"Oh, yeah? What do you call it then?" she asked.

"Passion," he said and then realized the trap he'd walked himself into.

"Exactly." A self-satisfied smirk crossed her features.

"You don't have to gloat," he teased, thinking he might need to have a one-on-one conversation with Hotshot at some point if the guy didn't get the message.

"But you walked yourself right into that one." Her laughter was all the music he needed. And yet, when she started strumming the guitar and belting out one of her songs, he realized how wrong he was for a second time tonight.

One thing was certain, someone with a talent like hers needed to share it with as many folks as possible. She had a rare gift.

All he could do at this point, was lean back and enjoy it.

"What time is it?"

"Ten o'clock." It was long past dark before Brax realized how long he'd been in the loft with Raleigh. He could listen to her all day.

"Oh, wow." She shook her head. "Sorry for keeping you up here so long."

"Are you kidding me? I just had hours and hours of a private concert with the one and only Raleigh Perry. I should be thanking you," he said with a wink.

She shook her head and smiled.

"Sometimes, like tonight, I just get lost in the music," she admitted.

"Was that new?" he asked.

"Just made it up tonight." She caught his gaze. "I was inspired."

She set the guitar down and stretched out her arms.

"It was incredible." He couldn't hold back the admiration. Her talent was beyond anything he'd ever experienced. She was beyond anyone he'd ever known. And he needed to stop himself right there before he went all 'fan boy' on her. Suffice it to say, his respect for her grew leaps and bounds after spending time with her.

"It's been a hot minute since that's happened," she said, and then looked around. "Being here brings out the best in me."

"I don't know. That was pretty awful when I really think about it." He couldn't help but tease her.

She crawled over on her knees just to tap him on the shoulder. "That's not fair. I'd never call you a bad cattle rancher," she said.

"How would you know one way or the other?"

She sat back on her heels and made a face at him. Then her hands came up in the surrender position. "You got me there."

Brax noticed the exact moment the air in the room changed. It went from light and fun teasing to crackling electricity in a heartbeat.

"May I kiss you?" he asked, looking into emerald eyes that glittered with what looked a whole lot like need.

"Thought you'd never ask." She met him halfway.

When their lips touched, one word came to mind...*home.*

This situation was impossible. There was no future. But they had right now.

Brax was on his knees in two seconds, his hands cupping her cheeks as he drove his tongue inside her mouth. The dark roast taste was long gone but he didn't mind.

She looped her arms around his neck and tangled her fingers in his hair, urging him to deepen the kiss. She nipped at his bottom lip, scraping across it with her teeth. All he could say was, *damn.*

Kissing her was right up there at the top of the best things in his life. It had nothing to do with her being a rising star. This was Raleigh from Lone Star Pass. A beautiful and intelligent woman who was sexy as all get out. A person who made him want things he probably shouldn't as he dropped his hands so they could roam her incredible body.

She pressed her body flush with his and a tidal wave of need welled up inside him.

Before things got too out of hand, he pulled on all his willpower to break apart. He found her forehead with his and tried to catch his breath. He'd never gone from zero to a hundred and twenty before like he just had with her.

The whole situation left his body aching for more.

"Hardy's still waiting," she finally said.

"Then, we should go," was all he managed to say.

RALEIGH KISSED BRAX FIREBRAND, her childhood crush. Seriously? More than once today but that session in the loft just now was beyond hot. If only she could go back and tell her sixteen-year-old self this would happen…nah. Sixteen-year-old Raleigh would never believe it.

Plus, she'd spent most of her time daydreaming about a singing career.

Brax reached for her hand as they walked out of the barn, and then linked their fingers. There was something incredibly sexy about holding this man's hand. Something that sent her stomach into a flipflop routine that would make any gymnast show a little respect.

At the back door of the main house, he let go long enough to open the door for her.

"I'll return this to Corbin," he said, holding up the guitar.

"Think he'd mind if I borrowed it for the rest of the night?" Being in the loft with Brax gave her a whole lot of inspiration for new songs. "I'm not ready to turn in yet."

"You haven't eaten dinner yet," he pointed out.

"True. When I get in a zone, I sometimes forget the basics. Food. Water." She couldn't remember the last time someone noticed whether or not she'd had a meal. Normally, she was making sure the band had a pizza. The past few hours had been freeing on so many levels she couldn't begin to unpack them all. What she could say definitively was that Brax Firebrand was good for her music.

"Why don't we set up in the kitchen for a minute and I'll heat a few plates," he said.

"How about you let me help this time?" she asked.

"You're a guest. No dice," he teased.

"I'm practically family. I grew up here," she countered.

"Fine. You get the drinks," he said.

"Are you hungry, Hardy?" She should have stopped at some point while in the loft and told him to go eat.

"Mrs. Firebrand brought me a meatball sandwich," he said. "I'm good to go."

Of course, she did. The woman was Raleigh's role model and superhero wrapped up in one adorable Italian package.

"Since we're inside the house now and I have Brax here, why don't you go power down in your room?" she asked.

Hardy took in the layout. He studied Brax, looking like he was sizing him up.

"How about this? I'll lock the backdoor," Brax said. He seemed to understand Hardy's hesitation.

Hardy nodded. "I'll double-check windows and doors on the ground floor before heading to my quarters."

"I can show you to your room whenever you're ready," Brax said.

Hardy nodded his appreciation. He didn't get close to anyone on tour. And yet, she sensed that he liked Brax. Or the Firebrands at the very least.

Brax locked the back door, as promised. Hardy saluted before making his way through the rooms, checking locks and securing windows. In the middle of June no one left windows open in Texas. It was too hot outside and most places had central air conditioning.

"I know Hardy appreciates the gesture," she said, motioning toward the door. "And so do I."

"He's just trying to do his job. I see no reason to get in the way of that," Brax said as he moved to the fridge. "Now, let's see what kind of leftovers are in here."

"I could eat your mother's meatballs three meals a day." She put her hands up like she was swearing on a Bible. "It's true."

"It'd be real hard to top that. But, let's see what else I have up my sleeve." He pulled out a container. "If memory serves, sour cream chicken enchiladas were your favorite."

"They barely edge out chicken fried steak, though," she said.

Road food was nothing in comparison to Mom Firebrand's cooking. No contest there. Raleigh knew all the best truck stops along the highway but there was something special about home cooking that no roadside diner could top.

Or maybe being home made everything better, including the food.

"Who had access to the stage on the day of your last concert?" Brax's question came after a long moment of silence while he prepared plates. He walked over and set them down on the table as she placed the water glasses down.

"Everyone in the band, of course. The crew and any onsite workers. Each venue provides a skeleton crew for a price." She sat down. "Oh, and my business manager, Wade."

"Have I met him?" he asked.

"No. As a matter of fact, he's supposed to be here. I called to check on him and he hasn't called me back." She fished her phone out of her back pocket and then checked the screen. "Still no word from him."

She opened her e-mail.

"Nothing there either." She glanced up in time to see the confusion on his face. "He's supposed to send me my financials."

"Do you have your account logins and passwords?" he asked.

"I probably have a few, not all though," she admitted. "I could be better about learning the business end."

"It's important to know all aspects of your business," he said.

"I had an amazing business manager until she left the tour to have a family." Raleigh had never wanted those things. The first time she really considered them came when Sharon broke the engagement news to Raleigh. As happy as she was for her best friend, a piece of her—the not-so-good-of-a-friend part—knew how much she would miss her partner-in-crime. "I never once had to question books or what was happening on the business end."

Would the bomb threat have happened on Sharon's watch? For reasons Raleigh couldn't explain, she doubted it.

"Sharon was thorough in everything she did. She was the first person at a venue and the last person to leave," she continued.

Brax didn't immediately speak. He seemed to take it all in and consider her words. If she had someone like him on tour and managing her business, she could focus on what she loved doing...

"Let me know if you're ever in the mood for a change of pace. I'd be beyond grateful to have a partner like you," she said on impulse.

11

"Afraid being a cattle rancher is in my blood." Brax appreciated the offer and he could immediately sense that she was only half joking based on the serious look in her eyes.

"I figured as much," she said with a wink. "It was worth a shot."

"I do know a thing or two about balancing books. And we have an accountant who takes a look at everything. I could have him review yours," he offered.

"Yes, please. I don't want Wade to think that I don't trust him but..." She flashed eyes at Brax. "I don't trust him."

"Give me his information. I'll have our person contact Wade directly. Might get a faster response that way." Most people who weren't qualified to do a job reacted poorly to a little outside pressure. Brax had a feeling Wade was probably dropping the ball and afraid to come clean about his mistakes at a minimum. It wouldn't make sense for him to be the bomber because he'd be out of a job if anything happened to Raleigh.

She took a screenshot, asked for his phone number, and sent over the requested information.

Brax forwarded the shot to his accountant, Manny Ortega.

He watched as Raleigh bit back several yawns in between bites of food.

"It's been a long, intense day. You must be tired," Brax said. "Let's get you upstairs and to bed."

He heard the way that sounded and couldn't help but laugh.

"Not exactly what I meant," he clarified.

"You can't take it back now," she teased as a male voice cleared his throat.

They both turned to the hallway.

"Kenny, what are you still doing up?" she asked, trying to come off as breezy. The atmosphere in the room changed and her shock at the interruption came across loud and clear.

"Came down for a glass of water," he said, looking none too thrilled to find Brax and Raleigh alone in the kitchen. His sour expression could be attributed to walking in during the tail end of their conversation.

"Glasses are in the cabinet," Brax motioned next to the sink. "Help yourself."

"I'd hate to interrupt whatever it is you got going on in here," Kenny said. Brax had seen a similar expression in his teen years when the opposing high school lost the biggest football matchup of the season on their mistake.

"We had a late dinner." At least Raleigh held her ground. "I'm not sure if the two of you have been properly introduced. Brax is one of my dearest friends from back when I lived in Lone Star Pass and we were just reliving old times."

"Must not have been very great, seeing how you couldn't

wait to get out of here," Kenny mumbled as he walked over to the cabinet.

Brax had half a mind to call the guy out on his immature behavior, but it wasn't his place. He didn't have any designs on Raleigh. She'd been clear on that point. And he didn't figure she would appreciate him being rude to someone in her band.

"There's a big difference between running from and running toward," he said by way of explanation.

"She told me all about it when we dated." Kenny's tone set Brax's blood to boiling.

But this wasn't high school and Brax could be the bigger person here. Besides, Raleigh would never go for someone who didn't respect her. She might have made a mistake with this guy once when she was much younger. She was far too savvy now.

In fact, he respected her even more for her mental toughness. She'd always known what she wanted and wasn't one bit afraid to go for it. The trait was admirable.

Kenny, on the other hand, sent up red flags.

Would he tamper with the stage? What would he have to gain? Did he believe he could frighten Raleigh into a relationship? Be her shoulder to cry on while on tour? Weasel his way back into her life?

It might be a stretch but was worth considering. Brax figured the FBI would cover that ground if they hadn't already. There was probably no way to get an update from them. Meeting the other band members and crew one-on-one became his next priority. He also needed to ask if she had meet-and-greets with fans before shows.

Would he be able to speak to the venue manager? Get a sense of what security protocols were in place. She'd been playing larger venues but that didn't necessarily mean safer.

Finally, he wanted to meet Wade. Brax could tell a lot about a person by looking them in the eye.

Raleigh rinsed off the dishes as Brax fired off a few texts to see what he could get going on his end. The last name Firebrand was capable of moving mountains in Texas. Brax had never thrown the family weight around until now. He sent off a text to the family lawyer to get him riled up.

Time to shake the cage and see what fell out. In the meantime, he planned to stick as close to Raleigh as she would allow.

"You could make an attempt to be nice, Kenny. After all, this family is important to me," Raleigh whispered. The exacerbation in her voice told him she was tired of going down this road with the man.

"What did I do?" Kenny threw his arms up.

The man was no threat to Brax. *Whoa there.* Where did that come from?

Brax ignored it and moved on. Kenny had burned Raleigh once. She had a long memory and a short fuse when it came to putting up with someone's antics. Break trust with her and it was game over. He'd seen it at school, and he was guessing that it was the same now.

He waited patiently as she finished up and then turned on the dishwasher.

"Don't leave your glass lying around for someone else to pick up, Kenny," she said. "This isn't the tour bus and there are other people living here."

"Fine. Maybe we should go back to your place or the tour bus," he quipped with a side glance toward Brax. "Who says this place is safer anyway?"

"I do, for one. Hardy agrees," Raleigh said. "But look, no one can keep you here. If you think you'd be better off on your own, take off. Wade can text you once it's safe to get back on tour and you can join us on the road. The feds did a great job of taking down everyone's contact information after the interviews. They know how to find you if they have more questions." She crossed her arms over her chest and turned toward Kenny like she was daring him to go.

"Nice, Raleigh. So...what? Now, you just don't care what happens to anyone else?" Kenny asked, sounding like a broken-hearted teenager.

"Interpret it however you want," she fired back. "You will anyway."

"Why don't you spell it out for me," he taunted. "Do you want me here or not?"

"Are you part of the band?" She turned the tables.

"You know I am." He shot another one of those sideways glances toward Brax. Was he checking to see if Brax intended to interfere?

If Kenny stayed in his lane there'd be no reason for Brax to stick his nose in band business. Not to mention the fact Raleigh was proving more than capable of handling herself. Unless she signaled for help, Brax was fine being an observer. It was more fun than it should be to watch the guy strike out.

Brax pulled up the venue on his cell phone, and then studied the layout.

"Then why would I want you to go anywhere?" she asked. "But I'm not here to make anyone else uncomfortable either. If you don't like staying at the Firebrands' place you can go back to the bus."

"What about us?" he demanded.

"We're bandmates, Kenny," she shot back.

"Is that all I am to you?" His frustration was evident in his intensity.

"Everyone in the band is like family to me," she defended, softening her tone.

Kenny stormed off without another word. Something bigger had to be brewing with the guy. Any normal person would take the hint. Or their ego would kick in at some point. Rejection stung. This guy didn't seem ready to accept what was plain as the nose on his face.

"What's his problem?" Brax asked Raleigh when she joined him across the room.

"Sour grapes, I guess. He doesn't seem to like the two of us spending time together," she surmised.

"How about you? Do you like being with me?" he asked, and then immediately wished he hadn't.

"I'm right where I want to be, Brax." Her answer was the equivalent of a bonfire being lit in his chest, warming him from the inside out. And just like a campfire, it would burn out.

RALEIGH STARED AT BRAX. Her heart pounded her chest as she waited for a response.

"Too bad you have no plans to stick around," he said.

"I'm here now," she insisted, not backing down an inch.

"And you're sending mixed signals." He reached for her hand. "So, let me show you to your room."

"Is this about Kenny?" She was getting tired of him. Her bandmate's pressure, his constant need to argue...his insistence on the two of them being meant for each other.

"This is about me and you," Brax said.

Well, damn. She couldn't argue his point. One minute they were lip-locked and practically on fire and the next reality set in and one of them saw reason. To say the situation was complicated was a lot like saying Texas summers were hot.

"Just because we want different things doesn't mean we can't spend time together now," she said.

"Doesn't it?" His eyebrow shot up as he led her up the stairs.

It was infuriating how right he was.

"We already agreed no more kissing. Again," she said on a sigh. All the reasons they couldn't figure out a way to date flew out the window when his thick lips pressed to hers. He had the perfect mouth and when he broke into a wide smile, there was a show of perfectly straight, white teeth.

"Probably for the best," he stated with no conviction.

It shouldn't make her smile that he seemed just as affected by the decision. It did anyway.

At the top of the stairs, he walked her down a long hallway. Most of the doors were closed. There were two open at the end, side by side, with one across the hallway.

"How many bedrooms are there in this place?" Raleigh asked, not bothering to hide her shock.

"Too many for one man, I promise you that," Brax said. "Yours is here."

"Are you staying next door?" she asked. Hers was the very last one.

"That's the plan," he said.

She stood in front of the door, unable to force her legs to move. They should probably say goodnight, but she didn't want this night to end.

"So," they both started at the same time.

Both laughed.

"Ladies first," Brax said, faking a tip of an imaginary hat.

"You're probably tired. So, feel free to say no. It's just, I won't be here for long and I didn't realize how much I missed Lone Star Pass until I came back." The words practically tumbled out of her mouth. She stopped long enough to take a breath and try to slow her racing pulse. "I miss it here. The law will figure this out and we'll be gone on a moment's notice. I was just thinking if you're not too tired yet...well...I'm really enjoying your company."

There. She'd come out with it. He could do with it what he pleased.

"I don't need a whole lot of sleep, so that's not a problem for me, but I saw you clamp down on no less than three yawns during dinner." He caught her gaze and held it like he needed to see for himself she wasn't too tired. "Are you sure about this?"

"Never been more certain of anything in my life," she said. "What do you say?"

"As long as you're always honest with me," he said. "No secrets between us. I feel something for you that I haven't felt in a long time but that doesn't mean we have to act on it."

"Open communication between friends," she said. "And, Brax, I can use a friend like you right now. Someone who is honest and honorable."

He waved her comment off.

"It's true," she insisted.

He didn't answer verbally. Instead, he walked right past her and inside the room.

This made her happy.

Two steps inside the bedroom and she froze. "Wow. Okay, hold on. Why is there a sitting room in here?"

"The en-suite bathroom is the best. You should check it out," he said with mischief in his eye that she promised herself she would ignore.

"Did you come to this place a lot growing up? This is my first time anywhere but the kitchen," she admitted.

"No. None of us did. The Marshall liked his privacy," he said.

"I'm sorry about your loss, Brax. I know he wasn't easy to get to know, but he did hold the family together in a lot of ways," she said.

"He was a constant all right." He took a seat on the sofa. "And, yes, he was difficult to get to know. I don't really care how everything gets split so long as everyone can come to an agreement, which they need to do already and get this over with. There's no good that can come out of tying up everyone's assets in court. Or arguing until the cows come home."

"I can't say he ever warmed up to me but he never seemed offended by me either," she admitted. "Mostly, he kept his distance."

"Which is funny because Adam swears he heard the Marshall whistling your songs more times than he could count," he said.

"What about you?" She claimed the seat next to him, toed off her boots and put her feet up on the coffee table.

"Whistle? Yeah, all the time." He winked.

It was just like him to dodge the real question. And she was beginning to realize how much she'd missed home.

12

Brax hadn't stayed up all night for the joys of conversation with another person in his life. And yet, the sun was coming up and he and Raleigh hadn't slept a wink.

"People will be up and around soon," he said.

She stood up and opened the curtains wide. "Now I see why the Marshall had such a big house. So, he could check out this view from every room."

Brax joined her, standing shoulder to shoulder, and looking out at the land that was part of his soul.

Her cell buzzed. She fished it out of her back pocket.

"Look at that," she said, blinking in disbelief. "Wade is on his way. Says he wants to walk me through the financials personally. He should be here by lunch." She pulled up her inbox. "And there they are," she said. "Hmph. What kind of magic does your phone have that mine doesn't?"

"Mine has a lawyer's name and number. I'm guessing that's what got Wade's behind in gear," he said, thinking it wasn't a good sign her business manager wasn't as responsive to her as he should be.

"This is good. I can start getting my arms around what's happening with the business side." She stared at her phone like she half expected the message to self-destruct.

"I'm going to go out on a limb here and say you need a new business manager." Brax didn't normally get in involved in other people's business and this situation definitely qualified. Except how could he stand by when he feared she was getting ripped off?

"While I have time off, it might be good to put some feelers out," she said. She snapped her fingers. "I know. I have a superfan who runs my fan club. I can check with her to see if…"

She shook her head.

"No. That won't work," she said.

"Yeah, it's probably best to find someone independent. Better checks and balances that way. I can ask Manny for a recommendation," he offered.

"I'd like that a lot actually," she said.

Brax fired off a text thanking his lawyer for lighting a fire under Wade's behind, and then asked for referrals. The response was an immediate thumbs up.

He showed her the screen.

"Well, now you're just showing off." She leaned into him. Contact sent another jolt of electricity racing through him. He probably should be used to it by now.

"How about going downstairs for a cup of coffee?" He could use the boost.

"Give me five minutes to freshen up," she said.

"Take your time." He was in no hurry to share her despite a bone-deep need for caffeine.

True to her word, she was ready in five. They headed downstairs together after a pitstop in his room to brush his teeth and wash his face. Halfway down, it occurred to him they were wearing the same clothes from last night. Would anyone notice?

A couple of guys were sitting at the table, nursing coffees while chatting with Adam and Prudence. The baby was asleep in her mother's arms. On occasion, Prudence beamed at the little girl.

The image of Raleigh holding a newborn, correction, *their* newborn imprinted on his thoughts. He didn't even want kids. Maybe some point way in the future. Way down the road. Not now. Not this soon.

He performed a mental head slap as they strolled into the kitchen, hand in hand.

A few eyebrows raised but conversation didn't miss a beat.

The coffee pot was full and smelled fresh. He grabbed two mugs as she went for the carafe. They worked like a well-oiled machine and when their fingers grazed, her emerald eyes sparkled.

He tried not to think about how much it was going to hurt when the case was cleared and she walked out the door.

Raleigh introduced him to the guys at the table; Buck, Jake, Willie, and Tim. As she finished another pair came downstairs. They were Randy and Hardy. Kenny joined them last, looking just as cranky as he had last night.

"Good," Raleigh said. "I'm glad everyone's here."

She walked over to the table and sat down.

"We need to have a conversation about Wade before he gets here later," she said. "We'll have a decision to make."

A look passed between Tim and Randy that Brax noted.

Angel fussed, making the most adorable sounds.

"That's our cue." Adam and Prudence stood up.

"Don't let us run you out of your own kitchen," Raleigh said.

"Not a problem. This little one needs some playroom time," Prudence said as she gently bounced. She really was a natural with Angel. Hadn't Adam said something about her not seeing herself as parent material either.

Strange, Brax thought, because she stepped right in with Angel and had been amazing. If he didn't know better, he'd say she was a natural.

Then again, meeting the right person seemed to change Adam in all kinds of positive ways. Brax wouldn't have pinned his brother as father material. Heck, Adam would have said so himself. He'd committed to a single life after having his heart broken. Funny how much a day could make a difference in someone's life.

There'd come a day very soon when Raleigh would leave. Brax had a feeling he'd remember that day for a long time to come.

"I can check on—"

"Why don't you stick around?" Raleigh asked before Brax could finish his sentence.

"Since when is he part of the band?" Kenny shot off as he poured a cup of coffee.

"His lawyer is the reason I finally got the financial documents I've been requesting from Wade," she quipped. "He's also the reason Wade decided to show here. So, I'm inviting him to stick around."

She glanced at the faces around the table.

"No one had a problem when Randy or Willie's girlfriends came on the road with us," she said. "They heard us write new songs."

"I don't have a problem," Tim said. The others echoed the same sentiment.

Kenny stormed over and took a chair. "Then I guess I don't either."

"Good. It's settled," she said.

Brax stayed over by the coffee machine. He'd been sitting all night and his legs were sore.

"Will he be coming on the road with us?" Kenny asked. The rim of his mug seemed to become real interesting to him.

"If he wants to," Raleigh fired back. She knew full well that wasn't going to happen. Brax figured this was another way to tell Kenny nothing was going to happen between the two of them. Not now. Not in the future.

And if her words didn't convince him, the look she gave next would.

Kenny tapped his fingers on the table like he was counting to ten.

Brax remembered the look that had passed between Tim and Randy earlier when she mentioned the band needed to make a decision. Something was definitely up there.

"Do you want us here?" Buck asked, motioning toward him and Jake.

"Johnny on the Spot is a little too green to sit at the big boy table," Kenny said.

"Hey, lay off him," Randy intervened.

"What the matter?" Kenny taunted. "Afraid he can't stand up for himself?"

Kenny was a real jerk. He was also too self-absorbed and shallow to pull off the bomb threat. He moved down Brax's suspect list a little further.

He wanted to know what the look between Randy and Tim was all about.

"GUYS, I know this is a stressful time and tempers are up here." Raleigh held her flat hand as high as she could. "But if we bicker, it'll only get worse. We've been through tough times and made it. We'll figure this one out too."

A few heads bobbed in agreement. Kenny was the holdout, but he would come around. He was already at the angry phase. Last time he'd put his sights on her all she'd had to do was parade a date in front of him for him to get the hint. He was being a lot more stubborn now. This was a new side to him. She didn't like it.

"Most of us have been together fourteen years," she continued. "This is the only family I have left, and I know it's true for a couple of you."

Heads slowly nodded.

"I think we should let Wade walk us through the books and explain himself before we put his head on the chopping block." Kenny made a hand gesture of a knife smacking down on the table.

"Okay. What does everyone else think? Is that how we want to move forward? Because I'm having a few problems with Wade that need to be brought out into the open," she said.

"For instance?" Kenny continued.

"The fact he isn't on tour with us half the time anymore," she pointed out. "And then there's my grandmother's...*my*... place. He was supposed to be taking care of it. He knows how important that home is to me." She shrugged. "You guys saw what shape it was in. I'm wondering what else is slipping through the cracks."

"My direct deposit hasn't come through this month now

that I think about it," Willie said. He pulled up his bank account on his cell phone and showed it to her.

"I haven't even checked my accounts," she admitted.

Suddenly, everyone was on their phone.

"No deposit on my account," Buck said as Jake shook his head in agreement. The younger guy sat there with a sullen look on his face. Kenny was being hard on Jake again. She needed to figure out a way to put a stop to the harassment. Then again, Kenny had seemed unhappy for a while now. Maybe the band needed to call a meeting without him to discuss his future. She tabled the thought for now.

Raleigh pulled out her cell and double-checked her account. "Nothing on mine either."

"It's probably just an oversight," Kenny defended. At this point, he would argue the sky was purple rather than admit to the fact it was blue and they didn't have a chance to rekindle a flame that had burned out so very long ago. "People make mistakes."

Well, that was a loaded statement. So much for him catching on.

"My wife is depending on that money," Buck admitted.

"We'll get you paid." At least, Raleigh prayed they would. She sought out Brax and exchanged a look.

He nodded slightly and she would take the encouragement anywhere she could get it at the moment.

"Wade sent over some numbers. I'll get working on those," she said.

"The Marshall has an office you can use," Brax stated and gave a little nod. He wanted to tell her something? Had he picked up on something she'd missed?

"I'll get working on figuring this out right now." She fired off a text to Wade, asking for him to call her about the deposits.

The bomb situation was awful. There was no getting around the fact. This was, however, giving her an opportunity to dig into a situation she'd been ignoring too long. As had the rest of the band. They wanted to play music and let the rest work itself out. The days of Sharon having their backs was over. They were long gone, in fact.

"I'll let you know as soon as I know anything," she said to the group.

"Please make yourselves at home," Brax stated. "There's food in the fridge and it gets restocked regularly. Don't be afraid to take what you want."

"Much appreciated," Buck said; the veteran of the group knew how to set a calming tone. Buck was irreplaceable. If she had to give him money from her personal account, she wouldn't hesitate.

Brax seemed anxious to get her out of the room. He didn't feel threatened by Kenny, did he?

She needed to make it very clear that Brax was her guy. He was her 'friend' if that was the right word. Considering the way her stomach fluttered every time he was near, she couldn't pin him to that zone. But it was a start.

The Marshall's office was incredible. Not exactly her taste but it was definitely larger than her entire tour bus. There was a fireplace in the corner and a flat-screen TV mounted above the mantle. A desk practically the size of her nana's kitchen anchored the room.

"That's a big chair to fill," she said, in awe. She would feel like a five-year-old sitting in that massive leather thing.

"You can work on one of the couches if you'd like, I just needed to get you alone for a second." Brax's comment sent those butterflies aflutter again. The sincere look in his eyes said this wasn't a sexual comment.

"What's going on?" she asked.

"You need to speak to Tim and Randy separately about Wade," he informed.

She must've made a face because he quickly added, "They exchanged a look when you said Wade's name."

"Oh really?" That was news to her but then she'd been too busy deflecting Kenny to notice.

"Twice," he said. "There's something on their minds that they aren't saying."

"And now the direct deposit issue..." This wasn't good. It was so not good. "I'll talk to them."

"Try one-on-one, if you don't mind the suggestion," he said.

"Okay." She drained her coffee mug and then held it up. "Now is as good a time as any."

13

Raleigh walked into the kitchen by herself to find everyone where she'd left them. The smell of bacon filled the air now. She walked over to a plate and asked if she could have a piece.

"Applewood smoked bacon," Buck said proudly. "Grab some scrambled eggs while you're at it."

"This is amazing," she said. "I'll definitely be back for more."

Buck practically beamed. He'd never had a kitchen this size to work with before, and the man could cook.

She walked over to Randy. "Hey, can I have a word with you?"

Randy nodded.

"Okay if we take a walk?" she asked. She'd be damned if he didn't glance at Tim.

Brax was right. Something was going on.

"Sure thing." Randy tried to come off as casual but the crack in his voice told a different story.

She walked outside and he followed. Once they were far

enough away from the house and any potential listening ears, she turned around.

"I need you to level with me about Wade." She came right out with it. This wasn't an investigation where approach was everything. "Do you trust him?"

Randy cracked a smile.

"You always do come at a problem head on," he said.

"There's no point in dancing around the subject." Holding back wasn't her style. Except when it came to men, an annoying little voice in the back of her mind pointed out. She shoved the thought aside, but it resonated.

"Have you noticed the way he's been acting lately?" Randy asked.

"Stranger than normal?" The guy had always marched to his own drummer.

"Nervous," he said. "He's not usually nervous. At first, I chalked it up to the pressure of the tour. Booking bigger venues. Our music and name have been picking up speed here lately."

"You don't think that now?" She'd believed the same thing. The music scene had a real buzz about their recent material. There was a lot of anticipation, and pressure, on these next few releases.

"Not since I overheard him talking on his cell phone. It sounded personal and like he was in some kind of trouble," he said.

"Why didn't you come to me?" she asked.

"Your name carries this band. What if I was wrong and got you worked up over nothing?" Randy's question was sincere. It was obvious from the tension lines on his forehead he'd given this a lot of thought.

"So, you talked to Tim instead," she said quietly.

"All I wanted to do was verify that I wasn't going crazy before we brought it to your attention," he admitted. "See if there was fire underneath all that smoke. Besides, I don't make a habit of nosing around in other people's business."

"You didn't mention anything after the bomb threat. Why did you keep this to yourself?" she asked.

"The man is cracking under pressure, possibly in a personal bind, but strapping a bomb underneath the stage?" He shook his head. "There was no way he would do anything to hurt us. Anything happens to the band and he's out of a job."

His logic was solid but she still didn't like keeping secrets from each other.

"I appreciate your thoughtfulness, Randy, I really do. It means a lot that you would want to protect me," she started.

He nodded and she knew he came from a place of caring. No question there.

"Maybe the pressure has been getting to all of us," she admitted.

"You won't get any arguments from me there." He cracked another smile meant to ease the tension of the situation.

"This career feels like a runaway train sometimes, doesn't it?" she asked, realizing she wasn't the only one who felt this way despite her efforts to protect everyone else.

"I don't feel right complaining. Most folks would kill to be in our shoes," he admitted.

"True." She never lost sight of how hard they'd worked to get where they were or how far they'd come since those early days. "I know how grateful we are."

Randy nodded.

"We're also human and haven't taken a break in a very long time," she pointed out.

"Doesn't feel like we should, feels like we're letting people down," he said on a sharp sigh.

She pinched her arm. "Flesh and blood, just like everybody else."

"Superman." He flexed his arm and wiggled his eyebrows.

They both laughed.

"Your wife and kids don't see nearly enough of you," Raleigh said.

"It's been easy for them to meet up with me since we've mostly played Texas venues. Now that the kids are getting older, they'll start school and I'll see a whole lot less of them." Randy frowned.

"Seems like we should figure out a way to change that. And we should probably talk to the others to see if anyone else has been holding back on information about Wade," she said.

"I'd like that a lot," Randy said. "Tim knows what I do. He has picked up on the change in Wade's general disposition."

"At least we'll be able to talk to Wade in person. Before he gets here, though, I want to get a sense of what the others are thinking. Especially now that we know he didn't handle payroll." She'd believed her grandmother's property had been the main ball dropped. "I'm concerned about the money. We should be making more, not less. Do you think there's a chance we're in financial trouble?"

He shrugged. "I sure hope not."

She walked back to the house with Randy, thinking she needed to do more than open the financial document. She needed to call the bank.

"Let me make a few phone calls before we meet with the others. Do you mind telling them we should get together in an hour?" she asked, her hand on the knob of the backdoor.

"I'll handle it," Randy said. He put his hand on her shoulder. "Be careful with Kenny."

"He's a grown man. He can handle rej—"

"No, I mean be careful around him," he said. "I can't put my finger on it, but something has changed in him lately. He doesn't seem the same to me and he's riding Jake a little too hard. The kid is gonna blow one of these days and I'd hate to see the two of them get into it."

"Kenny has definitely had a hard time hearing the word, *no.* I can personally vouch for him crossing the line one too many times." She took note of the assessment. Randy was right. Something was off about Kenny this time. She figured the divorce was weighing heavy on him. In the time they'd been together forever ago, he always talked about marriage as being sacred. "Thanks for the heads-up."

"We take care of each other, right?" he asked.

"That's what family does," she agreed.

And part of that meant she made sure the business ran smoothly. She opened the door and walked into the kitchen.

BRAX SAT at the Marshall's desk. He needed a scratch sheet so he could run some numbers and was better with a pen and pad than an electronic device any day of the week. There were a couple of folders on top of the oversized, hand-carved oak desk. Nothing that seemed too important.

He pulled out a drawer and a file folder with his name on it caught his eye.

Only him? Why wasn't there a file on any of his brothers or cousins for that matter?

This was the Marshall's personal space so it felt wrong to invade it but the question started eating away at Brax...why did he have a folder in his grandfather's desk?

Curiosity had him drawn toward the file. He drummed his fingers on the desk, debating whether or not he'd be breaking any confidence by taking a peek. The contents of the file were clearly about him. Didn't he have a right to know?

Normally, he wouldn't go rooting around in someone else's belongings, alive or dead. There was no honor there. But then wouldn't the file be under lock and key if it held information the Marshall didn't want people to find?

Anyone could stumble across it here.

Now that the Marshall was gone, it seemed like Brax had a right to the contents. What if there was a medical condition he needed to know about? The Marshall would never leave a piece of the ranch to him and not divide it up among his brothers and cousins, so no threat of a surprise component in his will.

Was there a loophole he needed to know about?

And then he thought about how antsy his mother had been lately. Did her actions have anything to do with the file?

"Hey." Raleigh's voice cut into his mental debate. She stood at the doorway.

"Before you come inside, let me ask a question." He put a hand up, palm out.

"Okay." She cocked her head to one side.

"If you saw a file with your name on it in someone else's desk, would you take it out and look at it?" he asked.

"Absolutely. I'd want to know if I was in some kind of trouble or had something wrong with me that no one was telling me about. There are half a dozen reasons to look and the biggest one is that it has my name on it. Even in grade school they taught us to label everything that belongs to us." She bit down on her lip and shifted her weight to one side. "Of course, you could just go to the person directly and ask."

"No, I can't." He dropped his gaze to the opened drawer.

She must've gotten the hint because she mouthed, 'Oh.' "Well, then, since you're asking me, I think you have a right to know what's in there," she said.

"Rifling through the Marshall's personal files goes against my beliefs," he stated.

"It doesn't go against mine." She walked over and crouched down next to the drawer. She pinched it between her finger and thumb as she skimmed the others. "You do realize there's no oth—"

"Yes, I do," he cut in.

"Do you want me to take a look?" She caught his gaze and held it. Those sparkly emerald eyes of hers seemed to see right through him.

He covered her hand with his, ignoring the familiar pulse that came with contact.

"My mom has been acting different lately. She said something was going to come to light and that she needed to talk to me about it first," he said. "My mind has been spinning about possibilities ever since."

"It doesn't sound like her to keep secrets." She caught his gaze and held onto it.

"My thought exactly." And was half the reason he couldn't seem to let it go. "She's been conflicted over it. Whatever 'it' is."

"Look at that file and you might save her the trouble of telling you," she said.

"I'd be breaking a code of trust," he stated, glancing down at the drawer.

"Normally, I would agree with you. However, did you go looking for it on purpose?" she asked.

"No. I was trying to find a pad of paper because I saw something on your financials that bugged me and you weren't here to ask," he admitted.

Her eyebrow shot up again the minute he mentioned her financials.

"You came across it by accident. It has *your* name on it. The Marshall isn't here to ask and you found it in his desk." She shrugged and put her hands in the air. "Seems like fair game to me."

"I'm going to table this now that you're back." He closed the drawer, knowing full well it was going to gnaw at him from the inside out until he knew what was inside.

She stood up and leaned a hip against the oak. Lucky oak.

"What did you see on my account?" One of her eyebrows shot up.

"Wade admitted to letting your grandmother's property slip through the cracks, right?" he asked.

"Yes," she confirmed.

He pulled up the spreadsheet and then pointed to line item after line item of charges coded, Lone Star Pass House, and Lone Star Pass Property.

"Wade was flat-out stealing from me?" She blew out a frustrated-sounding breath.

"It would seem so," he said. "It's tens of thousands of dollars over the past two years when you add it all up."

"The spreadsheet shows positive cash flow if I'm reading this right." She folded her arms over her chest. "I wonder what's up with payroll?"

"It would be best to double-check the balance with your bank," he suggested.

"I was thinking the same thing." She fished out her cell phone and made the call.

As he listened, his fingers itched to open the drawer and pull out the file. Was it really snooping if it had his name on it?

Again, the thought of rummaging through someone else's desk hit him in a bad place. He was protective of his own personal space and the Marshall deserved the same respect no matter how much Brax wanted to open the file.

Raleigh ended the call with a sigh of what sounded like relief.

"The good news is that the band isn't broke. I've arranged for payroll to be pushed through direct deposits today." She smiled and those eyes sparkled.

"That is the first good news out of this entire situation," he agreed.

"The balance on that sheet doesn't match the one I was just told by a long shot. I need an accountant to go through the books with a fine-toothed comb. Takeover for Wade on a permanent basis," she said.

"You might want to lock him out your accounts for the time being," Brax suggested.

"Right. Good point. How do I do that without going in to the bank?" she asked.

"Call them back and put a freeze on the account after payroll is deducted," he said. "They could take a couple of days to sort through the books. An accountant would need time, but Manny should have a good suggestion there."

She got back on the phone and made the call.

"That was easy enough, after jumping through half a dozen hoops to verify my identity again," she said. "I should have thought to do it when I was on the phone a minute ago."

"It's done now. That's the important thing," he said.

She filled him in on her conversation with Randy.

"They were right to be suspicious of him," Brax said.

"I need to tell the guys payroll should hit their accounts tomorrow." She pushed off the desk and walked around it before stopping at the door. "You coming? I'm pretty sure I owe you a cup of coffee for this one."

He held a finger up and then fired off a text to get Manny working on hiring an accountant.

"If you're buying, I'll take an extra-large cup," he teased.

Her smile was lighter now and he was proud of the fact he'd helped ease some of her burden. Her band might be like family, but she was definitely the one everyone looked to for leadership.

"That's a deal," she quipped.

He joined her in the hallway and walked beside her. She reached for his hand this time and the jolt of electricity no longer caught him off guard.

His mother stood in the kitchen at the table, talking animatedly. The Italian in her came out full force as she talked with her hands. She seemed to be entertaining the troops as Adam and Prudence joined them.

"She's right in her element," Adam said as he stopped next to Brax.

"No signs of stress today," Brax agreed. Losing the Marshall had thrown everyone off balance, including their mother. He was starting to realize there was more to her stress and the pull toward the file became stronger.

She spun around as Raleigh handed Brax a cup of coffee. He thanked her and took the offering. The first sip was always the best.

"I didn't see you in the playroom," Mom walked over and wrapped her sons in a hug.

"I've been helping Raleigh on the computer in the Marshall's office," Brax said. The minute he spoke he felt his mother's body stiffen.

"I'm so proud of that girl, I could burst." She relaxed and put on a breezy smile.

Raleigh walked over to the table, no doubt sharing the news payroll had been made. She pulled up a barstool, sat down, and explained the financial situation.

Mom took Angel as soon as Prudence was finished burping the baby.

"I'll take her back to the playroom while the grownups talk." Mom was in hog heaven with a granddaughter. Her face lit up every time her gaze landed on that little girl. Angel was going to be one spoiled kiddo.

Brax talked with his brother while Raleigh conducted her meeting. Prudence headed upstairs to take a nap.

"Still no sleep?" Brax asked his brother.

"Kids feed all the time when they're on a bottle," Adam said. Brax had never seen his brother happier, or more tired, which said a lot considering calving season.

Mom came bouncing through the room, baby on one arm, diaper bag on the other. "I'm taking her outside before it gets too hot. I have my cell if you need me."

Adam practically beamed. Brax knew his older brother better than anyone, and he never would have pegged Adam for fatherhood material. Boy, was he being proven wrong. Babies must hold a special power—power he had no intention of finding out for himself.

"I'm going to check on my new bride." Adam wiggled his eyebrows.

"Too much information, bro." Brax refilled his coffee cup before heading back to the office. He reclaimed the Marshall's chair and grabbed onto the drawer handle.

Figuring he might as well go all in since he couldn't seem to stop thinking about it, he opened the drawer.

The file was gone.

14

Raleigh noticed the minute Brax left the room. The air changed and she missed his presence. She reminded herself not to get too attached. Except that he was everything that was good about being home.

And that was precisely the danger. He made her want to stick around.

It didn't help matters she'd written three songs in the loft with him last night. Being with him reminded her of so many little things she loved. The smell of hay. A horse's nicker. An endless summer sky.

"How much did Wade take?" Willie asked.

"I'm hiring an accountant to figure out the books. They're a mess and nothing matches up but I already froze our accounts after payroll, and we'll get a professional on the job who can sort through it all. Give us a better picture of where we stand," she said. "Honestly, I'm tickled we're not broke. We do have a good amount of money in the bank. I have no idea what's supposed to go out or come in, but we'll get a handle on it."

"Thank heaven for small miracles," Tim said, whilst Randy nodded.

"I feel like I should have been on top of what was going on with Wade. I apologize for letting you all down," she said.

The rebuttals were immediate.

"You did no such thing," Randy said to a chorus of similar statements.

"Thank you guys for saying it, but I do feel personally responsible," she argued.

"We're in this together. Any one of us could have questioned Wade or asked to see the books. It's been a little too easy to let you do everything," Willie piped in. "That needs to change. We're grown adults and we should be pitching in more."

Kenny was the only one who sat in silence, arms folded over his chest, chin down. Was he still wallowing in self-pity? She remembered Randy's warning. Kenny had been quick to defend Wade. The two couldn't be in league...could they?

There was only one way to find out.

"Kenny, you've been quiet. Is there anything you want to add to the conversation? Your opinion is just as important as everyone's." She hoped she wasn't pouring it on too thick.

"I'm just a drummer," he said. "That's all I care about and all I want to do."

Kenny made a dramatic show of slapping his palm on the table as he stood before walking out the back door.

"Why does he have a stick up his—"

Tim cut Randy off by clearing his throat. Randy glanced around the room like he just realized they were in mixed company.

"He's been off ever since the divorce," Raleigh

mentioned and quickly added, "not that I'm making an excuse for his behavior. I'm just looking for an explanation."

"Someone needs to remind him of his manners." Willie was normally the quiet one of the group, so his comment drew a couple of eyebrows. The low rumble to his voice said he was fed up with Kenny.

"I'll have a talk with him," Raleigh offered.

"Mind if I take a stab at it first?" Buck asked. "I used to have a temper until I learned to get it under control."

"You?" they all said in unison. All heads turned toward Buck.

"One of my old bosses took me under his wing after letting me know my options," he said with a grin.

"I'd sure like to know what those were," Willie piped in.

"Get it under control or get off his crew and take my reputation with me." Buck smiled at the memory. "I told him to take his job and shove it."

The group laughed, breaking up some of the tension.

"But he was right and my reputation for being a pain in the backside always showed up ahead of me. I had to stuff my pride in my back pocket and go back to him to beg for my old job," he continued. "He hired me back and put me to work right alongside him. I kept my mouth closed and watched how he handled people. Learned a lot from that man."

"That's a great story, Buck," Raleigh said and the others agreed.

"I've been around this business a long time. Maybe I can get through to him," he said. "Plus, I need to get him to ease up on Jake a little bit. The kid needs a break. He refused to come down to breakfast, which isn't like him. Now, he's off somewhere on his own. He needs to know we care."

Raleigh hoped someone could reach Kenny. The more

she thought about it, the more she realized his bad judgment and quick temper probably had a lot to do with what he'd been going through at home. Being away all the time would strain any relationship, even a solid one. Kenny wasn't helping matters by spending too much time with his groupies on the road. Being unfaithful would wreck even the strongest marriage.

"I really hope you can work some magic with him," she said to Buck. "And I agree that he's been too hard on Jake."

"No one would argue there," Tim said. "What started out as good-natured ribbing has gone too far. We can do better."

Buck gave a nod before heading outside.

Raleigh grabbed her coffee cup and walked over to the pot for a refill. Out the window, she saw Kenny pacing near the barn while on his cell. He immediately waved Buck away as he approached. Instead of leaving, Buck walked over to the nearest tree, crossed his arms over his chest, and then leaned back like he had all the time in the world.

She smiled. Patience won wars.

Raleigh excused herself, coffee in hand, and headed to the computer in the Marshall's office. She couldn't help but think it was a shame he had this huge house and no one to share it with after his wife died.

It seemed like such a waste not to fill this place with family, especially on holidays. Raleigh remembered the Christmas Eve she'd spent at the ranch when her nana got stuck in Houston with a freak ice storm. When she thought of warmth and holiday and family, it was the smells that had come Lucia Firebrand's kitchen she remembered. Cookies baking in one oven and a pig roasting in another. Mom Firebrand was at their massive island rolling out homemade pasta before dropping it into massive pots of boiling water on the stovetop, her red sauce simmering.

She sat down at the Marshall's desk, thinking those meals should have happened here. She tapped the space bar on the keyboard, and the spreadsheet filled the screen.

"Do you have a minute?" Mom Firebrand stood at the doorway. Worry lines etched her forehead.

"For you? Always," Raleigh said without hesitation. "Where's the baby?"

"Her mother took her for a walk." Mom Firebrand didn't take a seat. Instead, she paced and twisted her hands together. The bad sign caused Raleigh to sit up a little straighter.

"I need to talk to someone, and you've always been like a daughter, so I hope..." Mom Firebrand threw her hands up in the air. She signed the cross and blew out a breath. "Brax is not my son." She immediately whirled around and mumbled a familiar prayer. "But he is my son in here." She put her hand over her heart. "He's mine in every sense of the word and I've been keeping this terrible secret from him because I was afraid of losing him."

Raleigh needed a minute to recover from the bomb that had just been dropped on her. She didn't want to know this about Brax and she certainly shouldn't know before he did. Her mind snapped to the file. She instinctively reached for the drawer.

"It's not there. I took it." Mom Firebrand gasped. "He didn't see it, did he?"

"No. But he deserves to know." Raleigh dug deep to find a calm voice while panic welled up from the inside. Brax not a Firebrand? Everything about him was tied to being a cattle rancher...and a Firebrand.

"I should have told him, but *how*?" Mom Firebrand sank into a chair and it was like all the life force had been drained from her body. Her bones seemed to melt into the chair and, for the first time, Raleigh could see all the wrinkles in the older woman's face. "How do you tell someone you've loved and cared for and held in your arms since he was a tiny baby that he's not your son? Because the moment he was placed in my arms he was mine."

"I know you did what you thought was right for him and it's easy to see how much you love him, but wouldn't you want to know if you were adopted?" She couldn't bring herself to scold Mom Firebrand and it wasn't Raleigh's place to. Her heart broke for the conflict adoptive parents must feel.

Mom Firebrand shot a confused look. And then recognition dawned.

"He's not mine but he's a Firebrand," she clarified.

Raleigh regretted mentioning it. She was walking into a sinkhole of information she didn't feel she had a right to know. Mom Firebrand should be having this conversation with Brax instead of her and it felt all kinds of wrong to be sitting in this chair where Brax should be.

"He's the same age as Corbin, so my husband paid a guy to change the birth certificate," Mom Firebrand continued.

"I'm honestly at a loss for words," Raleigh said.

"About what?" Brax stepped into the doorframe.

Mom Firebrand winced and let out a yelp before scurrying out of the room. She signed the cross as she flew past Brax. The sounds of her hastening footsteps echoed down the hall.

Brax didn't budge. He stood there, staring at Raleigh when she wished he would go after his mother.

"At a loss for words about what?" he repeated.

Panic made it feel like she'd just licked glue. Her throat was dry and her tongue felt like it was swelling up.

"I-uh-um." She locked gazes with him as she jumped up. "I just can't."

"THAT ANSWER DOESN'T CARRY WATER." Brax spread out his feet in an athletic stance and folded his arms across his chest, essentially blocking her exit.

"It's not my place, Brax." She couldn't be the one to turn his world upside down. He might still be a Firebrand but that could have meant a lot of things. He might be his uncle's child or...the Marshalls?

It would explain the file. Had the Marshall arranged for the birth certificate to be changed instead of Brax's father?

Raleigh knew what it was like to grow up without parents. It had been pretty awful at times despite Nana more than making Raleigh feel loved and protected. She shuddered to think what her life might have been like without Nana.

But this was far worse.

"Let's go find your mother, Brax," she insisted.

"You know something and you're refusing to tell me." The hurt in his voice gutted her.

"I hope you know how much I want to." She couldn't meet his gaze. She couldn't be the reason he was in pain. He might think she could stop it but what she knew would only make it worse.

"Then do it, Raleigh."

A sob escaped before she could suppress it. She shook her head. Digging her heels in like this ripped her heart out. "Go talk to her. Please."

She glanced up in time to see the daggers. They scored a

direct hit and she could see their friendship would never recover.

"Your mom loves you very much," she said by way of explanation.

"Now you're defending *her*?" he took a step back like he'd taken a bullet, and then disappeared down the hallway.

If Brax put a move on, he might be able to catch his mother before she got out of the house. Raleigh's refusal to put him out of his misery was a gut punch. He thought they'd become close—close enough that she should know how much it meant to him to figure out what was in the file. And he was one hundred percent certain she knew the contents.

Having Raleigh and his mother in league behind his back felt like a knife jab. He had trusted Raleigh, and he wouldn't make that mistake again. When the investigation wrapped and she got back on the road, it wouldn't wreck his world now. Because he'd started to believe it might.

He would do all he could to speed the case along, doubling down if need be.

Mother was gone by the time he reached the kitchen. He stepped outside and caught sight of her scurrying across the yard.

"Hold on there," he shouted.

His mother froze. She didn't turn around, which didn't surprise him. Even from this distance, he could see her shoulders shaking. She'd been in an emotional state when she'd bolted out of the office.

Brax realized this news wasn't going to be good. At this

point, he just wanted to get it over with and move on. Get whatever it was out in the open where it could be dealt with.

He ate up the real estate in between them in several quick strides.

"Tell me what is going on, Mom," he said.

She put her face in her hands and shook her head.

"I don't know how to. It's been too long and I should have...but I didn't...and now...how can I?" She didn't look at him and he knew in his gut this news was going to be worse than anything he had previously imagined. And his mind had gone to some pretty dark places.

"Say it outright," he urged, knowing he could never fully lose his temper with his mother no matter how frustrated he became. "Get it off your chest."

"What if you..." She stopped herself, dragging out the last word.

"I can't offer any reassurance if I don't know what you're going to say, and I can't imagine you could have done anything you couldn't be forgiven for. You've been an amazing mother and I love you." Those words were absolutely true.

She looked at him with red-rimmed eyes.

"You aren't my biological son," she said on a hiccup. "Which doesn't mean that I love you any less than the others."

Brax watched as her mouth moved but it was as though she'd yanked the earth out from underneath him. The world started spinning and he had to walk over to a tree to anchor himself before he face-planted in the dirt.

15

Raleigh couldn't let Brax deal with the news he was about to receive alone, and he would want to isolate himself. Besides, she couldn't concentrate on the financials no matter how hard she tried. Her chest hollowed out after looking into his eyes and she had to find a way to make him understand there was no way she could deliver the kind of news that could rip his heritage from him.

She listened for his voice as she made her way toward the back of the house. Tim and Randy were still in the kitchen as she walked inside.

"Have you seen Brax or his mother?" she asked.

They pointed toward the back door in unison.

"Thank you," she said.

"Word of warning," Randy started, "Mrs. Firebrand looked to be in an emotional state."

"Thanks for the heads-up," Raleigh stated. She didn't have time to explain.

The minute she stepped outside, she saw Brax walking away from his mother. Mom Firebrand scurried off in the opposite direction and for a split second, Raleigh was torn. She wanted to make sure the woman who'd been so kind to her and Nana was okay. But she *needed* to know that Brax would be.

Raleigh cut left, following him toward the barn. He disappeared from view and she wondered if he would hop on Bullet's back and race out of there and onto the property. Her only hope was that he would want to stick close to the house considering the ATV driver had been so close to Firebrand property.

When she reached the door and there was still no sign of him, she exhaled. Inside, she scanned the open layout. He was nowhere to be found. Until she looked up and saw a piece of hay floating down from the loft.

She raced to the metal staircase and took steps two at a time.

"It's me," she said, figuring he deserved a warning as she climbed.

"Go away," came the response, his voice a low growl.

"No can do," she countered, slowing her pace. She could try to justify not telling him the news, but she hoped he understood why it wasn't her place to tell him now that he knew what it was. He *had* to know. Otherwise, he wouldn't be up here.

She stopped as soon as he could see her. A muscle in his neck pulsed. Gaze narrowed, lips thinned, the man looked like he could rip someone apart with his bare hands. The moment they made eye contact her heart lurched. The intensity of his gaze warned her not to take another step.

"Okay, if I keep coming?" she asked.

"No," he bit out.

Raleigh froze, unsure of what to do next. A growing part

of her needed him to know how sorry she was and how awful she felt for this entire situation.

"There's nothing you can do or say. It's family business and that means none of yours," Brax said through clenched teeth. His jab had the impact of a stomach punch.

Normally, she would be ready to fight back if someone came at her with anger. But this was Brax. He just found out everything he believed about himself and his family was a lie. It was impossible not to feel like she'd betrayed him in some small way but not telling him the minute she knew. The no-win situation weighed heavy on her mind and in her heart.

But what could she say?

"I'm sorry about—"

"*You're* sorry? Why on earth would you need to apologize?" Brax seemed to barely have a grip on his frustration. Like bottled up steam ready to explode.

"Forget it," she said, refusing to stand there any longer, unable to look at him while he was in so much pain and not be able to do anything to make it better. "I'm going to go since my presence seems to be making this already awful situation even worse and that's not my intent."

Raleigh looked up and caught Brax's gaze. He stood there, staring her down, not saying a word.

She tucked her chin to her chest to hide the tears welling in her eyes. And then headed down the winding staircase. The minute her boots hit the floor, she took off running and didn't stop until she was far away from the barn, any Firebrands, and especially Brax.

"YOU UP THERE?" Adam's voice drifted up the stairs.

Brax had half a mind not to answer his bro...half-brother.

"I'm coming up. Don't shoot." Adam sounded like he was only half kidding. Hands high in the air, he made it to the top step.

"I don't have a gun and you aren't the problem," Brax quipped.

"At least you're still talking to me," Adam said.

"Did you know?" Brax asked.

"Didn't have a clue and it doesn't change a thing between us as far as I'm concerned," Adam stated with the kind of conviction that said he meant every word.

"How did you find out?" Brax asked.

"I ran into Mom," he said.

It was a wise move not to plead her case right now. She'd had thirty-six years to tell him the news. Thirty-six years to find 'the right time' or 'the right way' or both, as she'd explained. Thirty-six years to come clean.

"I'm just going to sit right here, if you don't mind." Adam took a seat at the top of the stairwell. "We don't have to say anything."

Brax appreciated how well his brother knew him. And, no, he didn't want to talk.

He couldn't be certain how many minutes passed before he finally spoke up. Half hour? Forty-five? He flexed and released his fingers trying to work off some of the pressure that felt like a boiling pot with the lid still on.

"It's messed up," he finally said.

"I agree with you one hundred percent." Adam's voice was calm in the storm.

On the one hand, his father had cheated on the only mother Brax had ever known. Then, there was the fact his own mother had died during childbirth. How his family had managed a cover-up of this proportion was beyond him. He guessed the Firebrand name could move some pretty big mountains considering his own birth certificate had been doctored.

"Wouldn't someone have noticed an extra child showing up?" Brax asked.

"Our grandfather had a lot of influence. He obviously helped cover this up," Adam said.

Brax shot his brother a look.

"Have you ever seen anyone question him? Or anything that goes on here at Firebrand?" Adam asked.

"Not really. Not when I think about it." The old man wielded a lot of power. He had a good side too. One that employed locals and gave generously to charities in order to help those who were less fortunate. He pitched in for fundraisers and made certain the town had a proper Christmas celebration, covering all the expenses not raised.

All this and he personally had an empty house on the big days. Their grandfather was a man of contradictions.

"I can't wrap my brain around any of this." Brax issued a sharp sigh. "I've been your brother my entire life."

"And still are," Adam didn't miss a beat.

The barn door opened and a familiar chorus of voices chimed in.

"Anyone up there?" Corbin's voice cut through the air.

Eric's quickly followed with his signature whistle. "Hey, man. What's going on?"

Corbin whispered something unintelligible. Eric grunted an apology.

"Can we come up?" Eric asked.

They seemed to have locked onto Brax's location. They didn't wait for permission. They were already shuffling up the metal staircase by the time he told them they could do what they wanted.

"Free country," he said under his breath.

"So, is that how it is now?" Eric asked, feigning insult.

"I don't know what to think anymore," he admitted, hating how this news might change his status among his brothers. He was the bastard child, the mistress's son.

"All I care about is the fact you're my brother. I don't need a birth certificate to tell me that," Corbin said.

"You do realize we're the same age now," Brax said. There was no rhyme or reason for his announcement, except it bugged him that his second-born status was in question.

"Have you spoken to our old man?" Corbin asked.

"No. And I don't see a reason to," Brax said. "Him and Mom had thirty-six years to come clean."

"I would want to know what happened and why," Corbin said. He'd always been the quiet, serious one in the family, nose in a book during most of high school. Which didn't mean he was a slouch on the football field. Friday night lights was important in Texas and all the Firebrand boys had played on the team. All had been damn good too. All had been scouted by one college coach or another at some point. Most had declined the offers.

Football and family might be close to a Texan's heart but so was cattle ranching. Corbin had gone to the University of Texas at Austin for academics, not sports. Which was also the reason he handled most of the numbers.

When Brax thought about it, he probably should have Corbin look at Raleigh's books.

"I know I speak for the others who aren't home yet when I say this news changes nothing," Adam piped up.

"It changes everything," Brax said before adding, "to me."

Adam turned to face Brax, issuing a challenge with his eyes. "Do you think Prudence is less of a mother to Angel because of biology?"

"Did I say that?" Brax's response came quickly but there was a moment of hesitation after when he realized the similarities.

"Didn't you?" Adam asked, the hurt in his eyes stabbed Brax in the chest.

"Hell, I didn't mean that and we both know it," Brax stated, leaving no room for doubt.

"This situation is complicated, but I don't see a difference in how any one of us feels about you," Adam said, some of the tension had eased.

"Tell that to Kellan and the other side of the family. Once news gets out, they'll have a field day," Brax said.

"And we'll put them in their places," Eric responded. His hands fisted at his sides. That was one of the certainties about being a Firebrand. His brothers always had his back.

He couldn't help but wonder who had Raleigh's.

This wasn't the time to be worried about her. Not after that bomb had been dropped on him about his own family. The annoying voice returned pointing out that she felt like family...*his* family.

The notion was insanity in its purest form.

"I appreciate each and every one of you," Brax stated. "I mean it. In my heart where it counts, you guys are my flesh and blood."

"Same," the word was spoken in unison.

"It's not our place to tell the others, so we'll leave that to you," Adam said. "The only reason we know is the state we saw Mom in. We couldn't let her walk away without telling us what was wrong." Adam put his hands in the air, palms up, in the surrender position. "I'm not defending her, by the way. I'm sure her and Dad had reasons that are between you and them," he stated. "We stand behind and with you no matter how much we love our mom."

Brax held back the biting comment they should all check to see if their birth certificates had been tampered with. Their show of solidarity touched him in a place down deep. "I appreciate you guys."

"We love you, man," came another chorus.

"Love you." Brax walked over to the trio and embraced them in a bear hug. But his mind kept wandering to the way he'd treated Raleigh. Had he been unfair?

RALEIGH FIGURED it was time to rally the troops. She knew when she'd worn out her welcome and the time had come to move on. She closed down the computer in the Marshall's office and then headed upstairs to pack. There wasn't a whole lot in her suitcase so it wouldn't take long.

She fished her cell phone out of her back pocket and debated making the call for a band meeting. She could easily put a message in the group text.

A question nagged her. Would leaving put them in danger? Could they slip out of town and under the radar again? Staying in one place could end up making them more vulnerable.

She checked the time on her phone. Shouldn't Wade be here by now?

The text she decided to send was to her business manager. No response came.

And then Hardy poked his head inside her bedroom

door. "Raleigh, there's been a break-in at your grandmother's place."

"Nana's?" she asked before realizing she didn't mean to say that out loud.

"I just got off the phone with the local sheriff. He's at the scene," he said.

Could this day get any worse?

"Did he say how bad it was?" she asked, imagining the farmhouse in total destruction.

"It's probably just overzealous fans in search of memorabilia," he stated. He was trying to make her feel better but the thought of losing her nana's belongings threatened to pull her under. The house, the furniture, the knick-knacks were all she had left of the woman who'd saved her, cared for her, loved her. Raleigh wouldn't be half the person she was today without Nana's influence.

"I have to get over there and see for myself," she said as panic squeezed her chest.

"Not a good idea." He shook his head and gave her a stern look.

Of course, he was right even though it frustrated her to no end.

"They're bringing a bomb-sniffing dog over from two towns over," he informed. "The place might not be cleared for a while."

Raleigh plopped down on the floor. She picked at the carpet fibers, wondering when *this* had become her life. She needed to think because...

She gasped.

Wade?

Was he in some kind of financial trouble? Syphoning money from the band to cover bad investments of his own or a gambling problem, and now someone was coming to collect? Had he gotten involved with the wrong people?

There was no way this could be a coincidence. Could it?

"Have you spoken to Wade today?" she asked.

"I was just about to give you an update on him." Hardy bit hard on his back teeth. "He's been picked up for questioning."

"Oh. Where?" She thought he was on his way to the ranch. It would make sense why he was so late.

"At the border, heading into Mexico," Hardy informed.

So, her world really was crashing around her. And now she'd lost Brax too. She was certain of it after the way he'd looked at her in the barn. Had she done the right thing by not telling him the minute she knew? She'd believed so at the time.

Now, everything just hurt.

16

Brax stood outside Raleigh's closed door. He brought his hand up to knock. Then put it back down again.

Every instinct he had told him to barge inside and apologize for being a jerk. Would she even want to talk to him at this point?

Jerk was probably too nice a word for how he'd acted in the heat of the moment. To make matters worse, he'd heard about her grandmother's place being ransacked and could only imagine how much that ripped her heart from her chest.

He picked up his fist and tapped on the door.

"Who is it?" Her voice was steady. Was she covering?

"Brax."

"Go away," she said, still steady.

He expected and deserved that.

"Or, how about I come in and apologize? Either that or I can stand here in the hallway and shout it out," he said.

The door fired open, but she blocked the entrance with her frame.

"Say you're sorry and get it over with," she demanded,

all steadiness gone now. There was nothing but fire in those emerald eyes, fire and betrayal.

"I am. Sorry, that is. And I realize how much of a jerk I was earlier. I don't want to drive a wedge in our friendship over my family situation." Situation wasn't nearly strong enough a word for what he was going through but he wasn't one for dramatics.

"You *were* a jerk, Brax." She shot him a hurtful look that nearly brought him to his knees. "But, right now, I have bigger problems than losing a friend."

The word, *friend*, didn't seem quite right to describe his feelings toward her. But this didn't seem like the time to hunt for a better noun.

"I'd like to help," he said. "And I hate what happened to your grandmother's place. I know how much that home and the belongings inside mean to you."

He wasn't trying to manipulate his way into her room by saying the right words. This was truth as he saw it, plain and simple. But those seemed to resonate.

She spun around until her back was flat against the door, and then she sank down until she sat on her bottom. Her gaze unfocused like she was searching inside herself for a memory.

"I miss her so much," she said, looking like she was struggling to keep it together. Seeing the fiery redhead at her breaking point was a face punch.

"I know," he reassured.

"The thought of losing what little I have left of her is kicking my behind, Brax." She didn't look over at him.

There was nothing he could say to make her feel better on that front. All he could do was be there for her. He'd had his world turned upside-down too.

At least he had his brothers. She needed a friend.

He sat down beside her.

"I know," he repeated.

"It's not a fan. I don't care what Hardy believes," she said.

He noticed her suitcase out on the bed, looking like she was packing up.

"I was told Sheriff Lawler was bringing in a bomb sniffer. He doesn't believe it's a fan either if that makes you feel any better." Brax overhead a couple of bandmates talking on his way in to find Raleigh.

"Did you know my business manager is being hauled in for questioning? They caught him at the border, as in heading to Mexico." She folded her arms and stared at the ceiling. "How do we pick up the pieces now?"

"When I was little and the world felt like it was crumbling, my mother used to remind me that there's a season for everything. I live it every day here at the cattle ranch, and yet I still forget," he said, remembering how wonderful a mother he'd had in Lucia Firebrand. She'd always put her children's needs first and he was no exception. "She'd tell me winter means spring is near."

"I remember her telling me the same thing when I came home for Nana's funeral." She leaned forward, hugging her knees into her chest. "It actually helped a lot."

"There were plenty of times her saying has come to mind over the years," he admitted, thinking about the countless times his mother had comforted him or intervened on his behalf with his father—a father Brax wanted to strangle at present, which was exactly the reason to avoid to man. Not that Brax needed a reason. The two rarely saw each other while working the ranch, save for calving season. Even so, there were plenty of hands around for Brodie Firebrand to make scarce. In the past week, Brax could count the number of times his father had grunted a hello at him...one. He'd be offended but his father treated everyone the same. Brax wasn't sure why his mother put up with the man all these years but she had to have her reasons. But this wasn't why he was sitting here next to Raleigh.

"Since the whole bombing incident, life has been surreal. You know?" She glanced over at him and his heart ached for her.

"I can only imagine what that must feel like," he said, wishing there was something more he could do. He'd never felt so helpless in his life and it wasn't a feeling he cared to repeat anytime soon.

"It's just starting to sink in that someone is seriously trying to hurt me and the guys," she said. "I know I didn't do anything personally to make someone angry enough to blow us up."

"What about Wade? We already know he was cooking the books," he said. "It's possible he believes he was about to get caught."

"And that meant he wanted to erase me and the band so he could...what...keep all the money for himself?" She shook her head. "You think you know someone and then something like this happens."

"People show you the side they want you to see." Despite considering himself a good judge of character, folk slipped through the cracks sometimes. It didn't happen very often but was always a gut punch when it did.

"I knew he was bad. That's the most frustrating part," she said. "At least at his job. We were just always so busy and things seemed to be humming along. We always made payroll, so no red flags came up."

"You didn't realize he was capable of criminal acts and attempted murder," he clarified.

"No. Nothing like that. I shouldn't have taken Sharon for

her word. The thing is, I trusted her. She talked me into giving him a chance." She quickly added, "And I know she would never have asked me to take him on if she thought he was capable of anything like this."

"Let's hope he is the man law enforcement is looking for. He's in custody and it's only a matter of time before he talks," Brax stated.

"If he does." She seemed to have her doubts.

"A non-career criminal should crack under the pressure of an interview with skilled law enforcement." As much as Brax didn't want Raleigh to walk out the door, she needed this nightmare to end. "I've seen Sheriff Lawler in action. He's one of the best."

"I hope so. We need to make music. We need to get out on the road again and finish our tour." She visibly shuttered at the last part.

"Why tour?" He couldn't help but ask.

"For our fans and because we made commitments that none of us take lightly," she said, and he could see her defenses rising.

"Do you *want* to get back on the road?" he asked.

"That's not the question." She rubbed her arms. "We have a responsibility to our fans."

Brax noted the fact she used the word, *we*. Had she buried her own desires in life behind the band's success? Was there anything left for her?

A BOARD CREAKED in the hallway. The sound of footsteps coming toward them set off a wave of panic in Raleigh. What now? More bad news?

Raleigh stood up with help from Brax. She planted her feet, readying herself for whatever might come next.

It was Buck and he held a dish towel up to his nose. Blood soaked the rag.

"What happened?" Raleigh immediately moved toward him. Or, more importantly, what had Kenny done now?

Brax must have been thinking the same because his hands fisted at his sides and she noticed his back teeth clenched as a jaw muscle ticked.

"Had a disagreement with Jake," Buck said.

"You mean Kenny?" she asked for clarification.

"No. Jake." Buck stopped and checked the rag. His nose was busted up. "Look at that. The bleeding is better."

"Let's go downstairs and get you some ice first," she said.

"I wanted to be the one to come tell you what he said," Buck stated as they all moved down the hallway.

She nodded.

"His exact words were, 'Y'all will get what you have coming.'" Buck stopped the second Raleigh put her hand on his arm.

"It's an indirect threat," she said, looking to Brax for confirmation. Jake? Never in a million years would she believe Jake was capable of a bomb threat, or any threat to be honest.

"I don't know if he was talking out of his backside because he was angry or if he means it and has plans to follow through," Buck said. "Considering what's been going on, I didn't think it was my place to take a chance."

"Where is he now?" Brax ground out, his jaw muscle ticking again.

"He shoved me and took off running," Buck admitted, and it looked like it pained him to do so.

"I'm sorry this happened," Raleigh said. A shot of adrenaline coursed through her veins.

"Wasn't your fault. I underestimated him. That's on me." Buck compressed his lips and shook his head. "It's not a mistake I'll make again."

"Remind me about his background." Raleigh knew when she hired Jake that he came from a troubled background.

They reached the bottom of the stairs and to a quiet kitchen. She went to work fixing an ice bag for Buck with ice cubes from the freezer and a baggie supplied by Brax. She had to admit that the two of them worked together like a well-oiled machine.

"He suffered physical abuse from his mother's many boyfriends before the age of ten years old. The state took him away from his home and he was moved around in foster care. The reports came in that he was a good kid but didn't 'bond' with any of the parents or family members in any of his new homes. He never made it more than six months before his mother would clean up her act and the state would send him back to her," Buck stated. "If you ask me, she did more harm than good."

"Sounds like a terrible life." She remembered bits and pieces of the story from when Buck first came to the band and asked if they'd be willing to take a chance on the kid.

"I just thought if he was part of something bigger...if he had a real family like what we have with each other, and a job to give him a way to make a future that he'd be okay." Buck hung his head and his shoulders slumped forward.

"Not many people would go out on a limb like that for someone they barely knew," Brax stated. His tone held the kind of reverence and respect normally reserved for elders or a member of clergy.

"Maybe I should have seen it coming." Buck sounded resigned to blaming himself. "I've put everyone here at risk."

Raleigh knew all about blame. She'd been carrying that burden for many years. Maybe it was time for a change.

"You did a good thing in trying to help him," she defended. "You have an amazing heart, Buck. You couldn't have known it would turn out like this."

"The guys were too hard on him," he said, compressing his lips. "I should have stepped in sooner and it wouldn't have come to this."

"You don't know that. Jake is a disturbed young man if he set that bomb. I liked him too," she said, realizing he would have access to the stage prior to a concert. He had a pass to get him past security. "I thought he was doing a great job."

Buck nodded.

"He took off, right?" Brax interjected.

"Yes," Buck said.

"Are his belongings still upstairs?" Brax asked.

"I believe so. He took off in a fit when we were outside," Buck stated.

"What was his condition?" Brax fished out his cell phone and palmed it.

"I'd say he was pretty upset. He cursed all of us directly and said a few other choice words I'd rather not repeat," Buck admitted before glancing at Raleigh.

There was probably nothing Buck could say that would surprise her considering she'd been with guys nearly twenty-four seven for the past fourteen years, but she appreciated the courtesy.

"I'll let security know to watch out for him. Do you know if he's carrying any weapons?" Brax asked.

"No idea," Buck admitted.

Brax made a quick call while Raleigh helped Buck ice his nose.

"I've got this. It's nothing I haven't had happen before." Buck waved off her help, so she handed over the ice.

"Where is everyone else?" Raleigh asked him.

"Hunting after Jake," Buck supplied.

"Let's go see if there's anything to worry about in Jake's room," Raleigh said. She waited for Brax to finish his call. "Are you coming?"

"I better warn my family members to steer clear of Jake and call security if they spot him," he said without looking up. "Go on ahead without me. I'll join you as soon as I can."

"Okay." She turned to Buck. "Ready?"

"Reckon I won't leave a trail of blood." Buck nodded, so they headed toward the stairwell.

"Do you really think Jake could be capable of making the bomb?" she asked Buck as they climbed the stairs.

"To be honest, I don't know. If you'd asked me two days ago, I would have defended the kid until the cows came home." His face morphed into a half-grin at the saying and his timing of being on a cattle ranch. "Now, maybe they've come home."

Jake's room was the first door on the left, down the hall from Raleigh's.

"I know what you mean. I knew Wade wasn't doing the same job as Sharon but with all the touring and song writing it became easy to ignore the signs that he was abusing his job. Plus, I *wanted* to believe he was trying his best," she admitted. There were a handful of people in the world she could truly trust and only one name stood out that made her feel like she could truly be herself around him. And that was Brax.

"He hoodwinked us all," Buck admitted as they entered

Jake's room.

There was a backpack and a ticking noise.

Raleigh backed away from the sound. Buck took a step in between her and the bag as she muttered a curse. She reached for her cell phone as they moved toward the door without turning. She called Brax.

"There's a backpack in the middle of Jake's room and it might have a bomb inside." The minute she made it to the hallway, Buck grabbed her arm and made a run for it.

"Get out of there," he immediately responded. "I'm on my way up."

"Don't bother, we're coming down," she managed to get out in between gasps.

"Quick question. Are we one hundred percent sure everyone is outside?" he asked.

She relayed the question to Buck as they made it halfway down the stairs.

"As far as I know they are," Buck said. The ice pack got chunked and he lost footing halfway down, his boot slipping on the carpet. His arms went out to either wall and he was able to right himself before going down on his bottom.

Raleigh kept on without missing a beat, a half step behind him. Brax met them at the bottom of the stairs.

"Send out a text. Tell everyone to get out of here. I've done the same," he said. "No one is inside this place except the three of us and that's only for about three more seconds."

Buck wasted no time running through the kitchen, his hand clasped around Raleigh's arm, pushing her thighs to their burning point with Brax on the other side of her, urging her to run faster.

Once outside, she immediately texted on the group message.

"I just alerted Jake to the fact we were in his room. I forgot he was on the chat," she said, gasping for air. Her side ached and her lungs burned, but they'd made it.

"Everyone is outside and away from the house. It would take more explosives than the kid could possibly have on him to bring down a house this size," Brax reassured. She would have to lean on his opinion because she had no idea what they were dealing with or why.

Texts started rolling in as Brax urged the three of them to keep going until they reached the relative safety of the barn. The thought Jake had had full access to the property didn't sit well with Raleigh. "What if he places explosives in a number of places?"

"My thought exactly." Brax immediately moved to the stables and started opening doors. "Get the horses outside in the exercise pen."

Buck went to work, looking like a pro at handling horses and she remembered his wife and kids lived on a small horse ranch in North Texas. She thought about how much they must miss him and made a promise right then and there to change their schedule as soon as she could. He needed to be with his family. The others needed time for theirs or to find one, whatever stage they were in. Kenny's mental duress might have to do with the fact his marriage had fallen apart. Kenny was always going to be Kenny, but being away from home so much couldn't have helped his situation.

Raleigh didn't stop until all six stalls were empty and the horses were safely outside.

Then, she looked at her phone. She stared at the message from Jake for a long moment before looking up. "Jake says he hasn't been in his room since early this morning and there shouldn't be anything ticking in it."

17

Buck's head came up and his shoulders flew back. The older man was most likely thinking the same thing as Brax. Jake wasn't responsible for the backpack sitting in the center of his room with a ticking noise coming from it.

Was it a warning? Or was it the real thing? Other questions followed. Who put it there? Why? Was it meant to scare or destroy?

"No one is going inside until we know for a fact it's safe in there," Brax insisted. "I'll get Lawler on the line and see if he can send a unit."

The call to the sheriff was short and sweet. Lawler promised to reroute the bomb-sniffing dog who was on his way home and meet him at the ranch.

After passing along the information, Brax turned to Buck. "The kid might be innocent."

"I hope so," Buck stated.

"But I'm not taking any chances with any one of our lives," Brax stated.

Raleigh studied the back of the house. She twisted her hands together and paced. "It just doesn't add up."

"Wade is in custody," Brax agreed.

"He is obviously guilty of stealing from the band." She shook out her arms like she was shaking out the tension stored there.

"The man is no magician," Brax pointed out. "He can't be in two places at once."

"Maybe he hired someone to set up Jake," Buck offered.

"Anything is possible." Raleigh nodded. She thought about the break-in at her nana's. "It suddenly doesn't seem random that Nana's house was broken into while a bomb was being set up here."

"Distractions," Brax muttered. "Someone is playing one step ahead of us."

"At this point, I'm guessing someone tipped off people to our presence in town. The crowd at Nana's yesterday morning sure found us fast," Raleigh said.

"Not a whole lot of folks drive on the road in front of the ranch out this far unless they have business with us. So, it's highly possible the crowd alerted the bomber," Brax agreed. "Or this is some twisted joke by someone on the inside." His mind snapped to Kenny, but would he be that cruel?

"Someone breached the ranch. Nowhere is safe for us," Raleigh stated, sounding more resigned than anything else.

"Where is Jake now?" Brax asked, glancing around.

"No idea. I'll ask everyone to meet at the barn." Raleigh fired off a text.

"I have to meet the sheriff," Brax stated. "Go on ahead without me."

Brax started to walk away and then stopped. He turned around.

"Hold on a second. Has anyone seen Hardy recently?" he asked.

"He should have checked in with me long before now." Raleigh gasped.

Not good. That was not good.

"Let me give him a quick call to check in." Raleigh held up her phone.

She did, shaking her head after a few moments.

"He's not picking up," she said.

Others started filing into the barn. Tim and Randy were first. Willie was a few steps behind. Jake, Hardy, and Kenny were nowhere to be seen. The possibility they could be together struck a nerve. Brax doubted Jake would go anywhere near Kenny if there was another option. Their feud couldn't possibly be for show. Could it?

Hardy was a head-scratcher too. He had been right behind Raleigh without fail since she'd arrived. The fact he was missing in action sent a cold chill racing down Brax's spine.

"Still nothing." Raleigh stared at her cell. She shrugged.

"Hey, Buck, why don't you explain what's going on to the guys in the barn? Bring them up to date?" Brax asked.

"Will do." Buck nodded and then took off.

"I don't know where Hardy is," Raleigh said on a sigh. "I'm starting to get worried about him."

"It's understandable, considering he's been one step behind you since your arrival. His absence sends up a red flag," he agreed. "The sheriff will be here soon with the bomb sniffer." The fact Brax's family were in danger added insult to injury. "We'll be able to clear the house soon."

"Hopefully." Her eyes were huge, and he could see tension lines forming on her forehead.

"We'll find Hardy," he said, knowing full well it was a

promise he wasn't sure he could keep. Adam, Prudence, and the baby had been out on a walk. They were safe at his mother's place. Adam said he would await word from Brax before returning to the house.

"And what about Kenny and Jake?" she asked.

"We'll find them too," he reassured. It also occurred to him the two of them might not want to be out in the open right now where anyone could take a shot from the tree line. Granted, they'd have to be a good aim, plus account for wind at this distance. But he wasn't in the mood to take chances. "Let's head inside the barn until the sheriff arrives."

THE ENTIRE SITUATION WAS SURREAL, the news getting worse with each passing minute. Something was niggling at the back of Raleigh's mind, and yet she couldn't quite put a finger on it.

As she rounded the corner outside of the barn, an image scorched her brain.

"Brax," she whispered.

He stopped dead in his tracks. "Stay behind me."

She felt him reach out for her and tuck her behind him, essentially blocking Kenny from seeing her.

"Don't you dare hide," Kenny said to her. His voice was dark and there was a desperate quality. "Come out and face the music or I pull the trigger."

Kenny had the barrel of a handgun pointed at Jake's right temple. A bead of sweat rolled down Jake's forehead.

"Don't do—"

Jake's sentence was cut off by the butt of the gun being slammed into the back of his skull. The young guy grunted as his head jutted forward.

“Stop,” Raleigh shouted, trying to push past Brax, who was basically a steel door.

“No, you’re not going over here,” Brax whispered, his voice a study in calm, whereas she was running on pure emotions. He put his hands in the air. “Take me instead.”

“It’s too late,” Kenny stated. “I’m not getting out of this one alive unless I take her with me.”

“We can take off together like you asked before, Kenny. Go to Mexico where they’ll never find us,” Raleigh was desperate. She would promise anything right now if it meant getting Jake back safely.

“Not going to happen, Kenny,” Brax stated. “Let’s come up with another plan.”

Kenny jerked Jake around. The younger guy dropped to his knees. Raleigh lurched toward Kenny.

Brax caught her in midair.

“What do you think he’s going to do with you when you get over there?” he asked her out of the side of his mouth.

She jerked free from his grasp in one move.

“I can’t stand by and watch this happen when I can do something to stop it.” She bolted toward the fence.

Brax came after her. She could feel him right behind her but Kenny brought the weapon up, pointing it directly at her chest.

“Stop or I shoot her,” Kenny stated.

“We both know you won’t do that,” Brax countered, but he stopped anyway.

She might have acted on impulse, but Jake was young and her responsibility in many respects. No, it wasn’t ideal to play into Kenny’s hand, but what choice did she have? Stand by and let him kill Jake?

The minute the sheriff arrived, Kenny would bolt into the woods and take Jake with him. The second Kenny didn’t need the greenhorn, he'd shoot him and dispose of the body. The image of the sweet kid left in the woods for wild animals to destroy sent another cold chill racing down her spine. The image would stamp her thoughts for a very long time.

There was no way Raleigh could let that happen.

The word that had been niggling at the back of Raleigh's mind surfaced...distraction.

Kenny had been trying to pressure her into dropping the rest of the band. When that didn't work, he'd hit on her. And kept pressuring her all the while ripping her and the band off financially.

All of which was one big distraction. With Kenny's constant pressure, she was keen to walk the other way when he approached, giving him a wide berth and plenty of freedom to do whatever he wanted behind her back.

"I'm here right now, Kenny." She stood at the fence. "Let Jake go."

Jake's eyes were red-rimmed but he held it together. He shouldn't have to go through this. Not after the abuse he'd suffered growing up. White-hot anger ripped through her when she really looked at Kenny. At what he'd become.

"Take the little jerk." Kenny picked Jake up by his shirt and tossed him toward the fence.

Raleigh saw the plan in Jake's eyes moments before he executed it and far too late to stop him.

Jake hopped to his feet and performed a back-wheel-kick. His heel connected with the weapon in Kenny's hand. The gun went flying. Raleigh scrambled over the fence as she heard Brax charging from behind.

Raleigh launched herself toward Kenny as he dove toward the weapon. She stretched her arms out as far as she could for Kenny as she lurched forward. He ducked out of her grasp and she landed on the hard clay earth with a thud. Her foot twisted underneath her and she felt her ankle snap.

There was no time to worry about an injury. Kenny was fighting Jake.

Brax easily hopped the wooden fence as the others came out. Confusion as to what was happening was stamped all over their faces. But the second recognition dawned, they were scrambling to get over the fence.

Kenny went down easily the second Brax entered the scene. With a grunt, Brax picked Kenny up and then tossed him back down on the ground like he was a ragdoll. Kenny's limp body slammed to the earth as Brax dropped down, pressing his knee in the center of Kenny's back. In the next second, Kenny's arms were being jerked up behind his back.

"The sheriff is here," Jake shouted.

Raleigh tried to move toward the weapon, but nearly passed out from the pain in her ankle. Anger roared through her as she tried to process Kenny's betrayal, and couldn't fathom it. They'd been family for fourteen years. They'd been a couple. How could he have changed so much that she didn't recognize him anymore?

Relief washed over her and through her as she realized it was over. The threat was gone. She could get back to her life again. *Her life*?

Raleigh wouldn't touch that with a ten-foot pole, except to say that making music was her life. The rest of the guys were safe now that Kenny had been caught. Kenny in league with Wade? Her brain was still having a hard time processing the betrayal, but at least they knew what they were dealing with now. No more bombs. No more threats of dying.

Raleigh could finally exhale. She inched toward Brax, nearly passing out from the pain in her ankle.

"You're okay. Stay right there," Brax's calm masculine, whiskey over ice cream voice washed over her and through her. "Help is on the way."

Sheriff Lawler came running. He had fair skin, and ginger hair in a military cut. He had a hawk-like nose and compassionate honey-brown eyes. He wore jeans, boots, and a tan shirt with the word, *Sheriff*, embroidered on the right front pocket.

The lawmen immediately took over for Brax, who gave the elevator version of what just went down before rushing toward Raleigh. She managed to sit up, with his help, wincing as she moved her ankle. Jake made his way over, looking pretty busted up. His mouth was bleeding as was his nose, but he shook it off.

"I don't know how to thank you," he started, but Brax waved him off.

"You're part of the family now. That's what families do for each other," Brax said as Jake used the fence post to support himself.

The sheriff read Kenny his rights as Brax pressed a tender kiss to Raleigh's lips.

"We're okay," he whispered.

"This scumbag is going to spend the rest of his life behind bars for attempted murder," Sheriff Lawler said, forcing Kenny to stand. Lawler looked at Raleigh. "Your business manager is willing to testify that Kenny here has been pressuring him to syphon money from the band. Kenny believes that he's the reason for the band's success. Therefore, he has rights to take the money and you, Ms. Perry."

Raleigh grunted. "He doesn't deserve me or the band. We were his family and this is how he treated us."

Head low, Kenny didn't look over at her. It was probably a good thing because it seemed to be taking all of Brax's willpower not to take Kenny down personally.

Brax studied Jake.

"He's not worth going to jail for. Or, believe me, I would have already done what you're thinking," Brax stated.

Jake relaxed his fisted hands and nodded as EMTs rushed the scene.

Seeing the interaction between the two of them caused Raleigh's chest to squeeze and a dozen campfires to light inside her. She couldn't be happier this whole nightmare was over. But where did that leave her and Brax?

18

There was a whole lot on Brax's mind as he watched the EMT as he finished wrapping Raleigh's ankle. Thankfully, it was a bad sprain, not broken. The very real thought he'd almost lost her sucked the air from his lungs. Taking in a breath hurt and his chest cramped.

Sheriff Lawler came jogging over.

"There is no bomb. Thought I'd deliver the news personally," he said.

"What was it then?" Brax asked as relief washed over him. He exchanged a glance with Raleigh and saw the same reaction.

"One of those alarm clocks that makes a ticking noise," Lawler supplied, his chest heaving. "Now, if you'll excuse me, I have a perp to lock up."

"Thank you," Brax said. "For everything you've done."

Lawler nodded, smiled, and then turned back toward his SUV in the distance.

"You're all set," the EMT said to Raleigh.

Now that she'd come back to town and made her way

into Brax's heart, he couldn't envision a life without her. It might be for nothing, but he had to tell her how he felt. See if there was a chance the two of them could find common ground.

His arms ached to hold her again. So, he cut a straight line right to her, catching and holding her gaze.

Words escaped him so he hauled her against his chest and looped his arms around her waist. She leaned into him and the familiar jolt of electricity rocketed through him as he looked into those beautiful eyes. One word came to mind...*home.*

He dipped his head down and claimed her mouth one last time. Saying what he had to might ruin their budding relationship. He had to risk it. He had to know if she felt the same way.

In that moment, nothing mattered more than the feel of her lips moving against his. She brought her hand up and grazed her fingers over the day-old stubble on his chin.

With heroic effort, he pulled back. He leaned his forehead to rest against hers as he took a second to catch his breath. This woman, this incredible woman.

"You are beautiful, Raleigh. And I mean inside and out," he began, hoping the words would come as he took a tentative step forward onto unfamiliar turf.

She smiled up at him and his heart took a hit.

"I thought I lost you..." He stopped right there as emotion stuck in his throat, jumbling up the words he was trying so hard to get out before he lost it. And Brax never 'lost it' with anyone. But then this was Raleigh. She was the definition of one-of-a-kind and he knew in his heart he would never come across anyone who could hold a candle to her. "I can't walk away. I can't live my life without you in it."

"Maybe you don't have to," she said, and it was the first sign of hope the magnitude of what was happening on his end might be a two-way street.

She locked gazes with him. He could stare into those emerald eyes of hers forever.

"What are you saying?" he asked.

"I have feelings for you that I've never experienced." She dropped her gaze.

"Not many people have the power to wreck me, Raleigh. It's you. Only you. You hold the key to my future in your hands because I'm in love with you," he said.

She blinked up at him like she was trying to grasp the implications of what he'd just said. For a few seconds that felt like minutes, he held his breath.

"You love me?" she asked, disbelief clouding those eyes.

"I've never loved anyone like I love you, Raleigh. You're incredibly strong. You have more talent in your pinky than most have in their whole bodies. You're smart. You're determined and you have the kindest heart. You don't back down from a fight either. You're special and—"

"Are you sure about that, Brax?" she countered, looking at him like she was searching for a head injury. "We have a history that goes way back and you've never shown the slightest interest until now."

"Why would I? The age difference was a big deal back then," he defended. "You were too young and, besides, I thought you were a real pain in the backside to be honest."

He couldn't hold back his grin at the memory.

"So were you," she fired back with a stiff elbow to his ribs.

"Not *that* young," he clarified.

"What changed, Brax? I feel something between us brewing too, but I have a career that means I'll be on the road tomorrow." She frowned when she looked at her ankle. "Or very soon."

"Is that what this is about?" he asked. "You leaving to go on tour?"

"That's a big part of my life and right now it doesn't matter if I'm ready to slow down. I have commitments and I won't let my fans down." The look of determination in her eyes said this point was non-negotiable.

"You wouldn't be you if you did." His grin was probably ear-to-ear but he didn't care. The way she cared about others was one of the biggest draws toward her in his book. "What if I said that I don't want a scaled-down version of the woman I love? And I don't ever want you to think you have to tone down your life to fit mine." The fact they were talking about this at all meant her feelings ran deep and she wasn't sure what to do about them.

"I'd say it's too good to be true," she quickly countered.

"I'll take leave from the ranch and follow you wherever you go," he said. "I want you to have everything you want in life and then some. Marrying me shouldn't feel like compromising in any way."

"Wouldn't you be..." She blinked up at him. "Hold on a minute. What did you just say, Brax Firebrand?"

He dropped down on one knee and took her hand in his. He'd never been more nervous in his life but he had a very important question to ask.

"Would you do me the incredible honor of marrying me?"

"Are you serious?" The spark in her eyes told him everything he needed to know about how she was about to answer.

"I've never meant anything more in my life," Brax reassured.

She shot him another warning look. "Because I think I've been in love with you my whole life. Even when I didn't even know what it meant all those years ago. I wrote my feelings off as a crush, child's play. But if this is serious…if *you're* serious then I'm willing to talk."

All he could do was nod and hope she believed him, and maybe string together the right words to convince her that he had never been more serious.

"All I know is that I don't want to take another breath without knowing we'll figure out a way to be together. And I mean really be together. Like a promise of forever and a ring on a finger."

"Yes," she finally said as a rogue tear tumbled down her cheek. "I'll marry you, Brax Firebrand."

Brax stood and kissed his future bride to the backdrop of cheers and a chorus of congratulations. He had his Raleigh. He'd found his home.

19

EPILOGUE

Corbin Firebrand lived by a code that said he always lent a hand when asked. But his oldest cousin's ex-wife should probably be the exception to the rule.

He checked the screen on his cell phone one more time before tucking it inside his tux pocket.

"Is that important?" Brax asked.

"It can wait," Corbin said, trying to play off the stress that was making his blood pressure rise. "What was it you said about hell freezing over before anyone would get you to think about walking down this aisle?"

"When you find the one, you don't throw it away." Brax's grin was practically ear-to-ear.

"Well, you can wipe that ridiculous smile off your face," Corbin teased. "No one wants to see that silly grin as you walk down the aisle."

"Hey. What do you have against me being happy?" Brax teased as Adam joined in. "Help me out here. Corbin is giving me a hard time for marrying the woman of my dreams."

"He'll understand when he finds it for himself. Before then, there's no amount of discussion in the world that will help." Adam threw a friendly elbow into Corbin's ribs.

What could Corbin say, other than his brother would have made a great soccer player.

Still, he had no idea how both of his brothers could be acquiring balls and chains within weeks of each other.

His cell buzzed again. He checked the screen. The familiar SOS signal caused his chest to squeeze. Liv Holden was sending up the bat signal. Was she even in town?

"Would you look at that," Adam said to Brax. "The way our brother is studying his cell phone means he might know better than he's pretending."

Adam and Brax laughed. Corbin didn't want to spoil his brothers' good moods. After all, it was Brax's wedding day.

When his cell buzzed for the third time, Corbin excused himself. He made it through the ceremony and lunch reception despite checking his phone half a dozen times.

The emergency signal glared at him. Call it cowboy code, but he could no longer ignore the plea for help.

Heaven help him, but he changed his clothes and hopping inside his truck. He could give Liv Holden five minutes and then he needed to make her understand she couldn't reach out to him ever again.

To read Corbin and Liv's story, click here.

ALSO BY BARB HAN

Texas Firebrand

Rancher to the Rescue

Disarming the Rancher

Rancher under Fire

Rancher on the Line

Undercover with the Rancher

Rancher in Danger

Don't Mess With Texas Cowboys

Texas Cowboy's Protection (*FREE*)

Texas Cowboy Justice

Texas Cowboy's Honor

Texas Cowboy Daddy

Texas Cowboy's Baby

Texas Cowboy's Bride

Texas Cowboy's Family

Cowboys of Cattle Cove

Cowboy Reckoning (*FREE*)

Cowboy Cover-up

Cowboy Retribution

Cowboy Judgment

Cowboy Conspiracy

Cowboy Rescue

Cowboy Target

Cowboy Redemption

Cowboy Intrigue

Cowboy Ransom

Crisis: Cattle Barge

Sudden Setup

Endangered Heiress

Texas Grit

Kidnapped at Christmas

Murder and Mistletoe

Bulletproof Christmas

For more of Barb's books, visit www.BarbHan.com.

ABOUT THE AUTHOR

Barb Han is a USA TODAY and Publisher's Weekly Best-selling Author. Reviewers have called her books "heartfelt" and "exciting."

Barb lives in Texas—her true north—with her adventurous family, a poodle mix and a spunky rescue who is often referred to as a hot mess. She is the proud owner of too many books (if there is such a thing). When not writing, she can be found exploring Manhattan, on a mountain either hiking or skiing depending on the season, or swimming in her own backyard.

Sign up for Barb's newsletter at www.BarbHan.com.

Printed in Great Britain
by Amazon

69875067R00111